BINGS DEH QUAKSA
AND OTHER STORIES

CLEMENT WHITE

authorHOUSE®

AuthorHouse™
1663 Liberty Drive
Bloomington, IN 47403
www.authorhouse.com
Phone: 1 (800) 839-8640

Published by AuthorHouse 01/13/2018

ISBN: 978-1-5462-1843-2 (sc)
ISBN: 978-1-5462-1841-8 (hc)
ISBN: 978-1-5462-1842-5 (e)

Library of Congress Control Number: 2017917914

Print information available on the last page.

Any people depicted in stock imagery provided by Thinkstock are models,
and such images are being used for illustrative purposes only.
Certain stock imagery © Thinkstock.

This book is printed on acid-free paper.

Contents

ACKNOWLEDGEMENTS

Endless thanks to my wife, Dr. Jeannette Smith White, who continues to inspire me. Her love and encouragement knew no limits. The confidence that she displayed in me motivates me to this day. To our children, Sekou "Chike" and Asha, and our grandsons, Amari and Ahsir, and granddaughter Avani ("mi princesa") you mean everything to me.

So much appreciation for my mother, Marjorie Margarita Asta White Stevens for uncompromising, unconditional love and support. Even though her journey on earth is now ended, she continues to guide me as she always did. She never attended school, nor read a book, but was my first teacher, with invaluable and life long lessons.

Ana Cecilia Rosado for your years of friendship, thanks. To Dr. Marta Rodríguez for your many years of support and encouragement, thanks.

To my sister Cheryl A. White, because of your dedication to our mother, I was able to continue writing. I recognize and appreciate your sacrifice. My brothers and I owe you a debt of gratitude.

Thanks to my friend, Edward "the Secret Weapon Charles" who after so many years away from St. Thomas, still remembers Bings—proof of his many days spent in Pearson Gardens in the 60's. To my Housin' buddy Dr. Sidney Rabsatt who still has P.M.P.G. in his heart!

To fellow and sister writers Habib Tiwoni, Dr. Gilbert Sprauve, Elaine Warren Jacobs, Dr. Vincent Cooper, Daisy Holder, Dr. Ruby Simmonds,

Larry Sewer, Tregenza Roach, the prolific Dr. Simon B. Jones Hendrickson, Edgar Lake and Richard Scharader, you are an inspiration to all Virgin Islands writers; your works have served as literary models over the years. Edgar, you are a brilliant scholar whose advice and guidance have been instrumental in my literary career.

Karla Crispín I appreciate your timely input, technical and organizational support. Thanks for being an extra pair of eyes.

Shirlene Williams Lee, from the very beginning in the 1960's you played a pivotal role in the transcription of my work, typing my manuscripts with your inimitable professionalism and expertise. Words are not sufficient to express my gratitude to you. Critic, poet, advisor, commentator, photographer, motivator, analyst, sounding board, artist, designer, and more importantly, friend—from the first grade at the extraordinary Dober School until now! You have been there every step of the way. Everything you do, you do it well. Without your assistance this project would have never been completed.

Lesmore "Dandy" Howard, James "Jaime Benítez" Hedrington, Tino Colón, Kwame "Mote" Motilewa, Marilyn "Tambi" Turnbull, much thanks. Kwabena Davis, I admire your respect for V.I. culture. Dandy Howard, your reservoir of Virgin Islands history, culture, and traditions is truly impressive. So much knowledge! Because of our 50+ years of friendship I have been the beneficiary of your knowledge, among the very best of the Ashanti storytellers. I consider myself lucky. Carol Henneman, for your love of Virgin Islands and West Indian culture, thanks.

To all our mothers in Paul M. Pearson Gardens during the 1950's, '60's, and early 70's, who sacrificed all so that we could grow up as solid citizens, thank you so much. Boys and girls from Pearson Gardens and Savan, thanks for your comradery. To the people of the Virgin Islands, and West Indies, in general, you have inspired me! Miss Chrissy Testamark, Miss Iona Henry, and Mrs. Viola Simmonds, your guidance and love were beyond measure.

Mrs. Viola Simmonds and Ralph Simmonds, the first people to sit and discuss with me my first collection, **<u>Wey Butty</u>**, I valued their insight and input. They were very special in my life.

To my brothers and sisters and my numerous nieces and nephews, all ah dem, thanks!

Miss Ruth Thomas, your guidance has made a difference in my life. How can I measure the impact of people like you on our community? Special thanks to Fiolina Mills for your many Spanish lessons in the 1960's. Thanks to Carmen Encarnación y Alicia Ortiz for their excllent lessons in Spanish, and encouragement. Recognition to Mr. Addie Ottley for his efforts in reviving and preserving Virgin Islands traditions and culture.

Mrs. Bernice Louise Heyliger, everyone now knows that without you, I would not be writing anything. Endless thanks and appreciation.

Cover artistic renditions by St. Thomas' great artist Roy "Naska" Hansen.

INTRODUCTION

I will begin with a paradoxical reflection: These narratives do not pretend to faithfully recreate Virgin Islands oral stories; yet, it is my hope that they engender some level of faith in our narrative genre. The notion of "faithful" stories is distorted by the natural process of oral elaboration. **Bings Deh Quaksa & Other Stories** is not biographical, but neither is it historical. Yet, it is a work with echoes of the past, traits of biography and certainly hints of the autobiographical, all centrifugally drawn into a vortex by the over-reaching arm of fiction itself. As children growing up in the Virgin Islands, we sat and listened to numerous stories told by masters of the word. The numerous storytellers in the West Indies are epitomized in my mind by the inimitable Butty, one of my many muses on St. Thomas.* Butty is in fact the metonym for the Virgin Islands' oral traditions. Orality by its very nature invites us to dream, to imagine, to create, and this should never be considered cultural heresy.

We are aware of the ever-constant modification and re modification of the "telling"—the relating of the narrative. Because of the shifting tendencies of the oral exchange these narratives do not aim to reproduce stories verbatim as we may have heard some of them; at the same time, however, they are deeply rooted in Virgin Islands and West Indian oral history, myth, beliefs, tradition, customs, worldview, and lore; in essence, in our culture. Ultimately, as fictional works, they must operate within the paradigmatic framework of the creative process, and not as some blueprint for "truth." Even history itself must submit to the scrutiny of the imagination.

Once again the question of language drags us into the inexhaustible debate of Virgin Islands Creole versus the so-called "standard" English.* But, it is a debate worth engaging in because in the Virgin Islands we are molded by multiple linguistic modalities. Culturally we are always negotiating two different, but at times tangentially linguistic paradigms, constantly engaged in a kind of "double consciousness," to borrow Dubois coinage. Ultimately, the "choice" of a particular vernacular in this collection is guided by the dictates of the creative impulse, and not by any inner quest for authenticity. The liberties granted by the creative process have been at the center of this collection, which admittedly mixes the process of writing with ideologies lurking somewhere in the deepest recesses of my mind. I hope that these stories serve to connect us to others, with those who also have stories, submerged somewhere in their subconscious.

In the process of connecting to others, it is my hope that the stories will reconnect us to ourselves. Who are we, coming from others, who come from elsewhere and who came from others, coming from elsewhere? May this be one possible step in the awakening and the unlocking of those closed reservoir of lost narratives of our cultural realities.

*See my exploration of this theme in my book **MEET MEH UNDAH DEH BONGOLO & TARK LIKE WE NO—A CASE FOR VIRGIN ISLANDS CREOLE DEN AN' NOW & A SOCIO-CULTURAL LEXICON**

For: Butty, who elevated the art of storytelling

For: Dr. Gilbert Sprauve, Mr. Corey Emmanuel, Dr. Lezmore Emmanuel, and Mr. Elmo Roebuck, great Virgin Islands guardians of culture and history—True Ashanti poets and storytellers!

FOR MY FRIEND/BROTHER, ALFRED WARREN, STELLAR
WRITER, MASTER OF THE SHORT STORY GENRE

FOR

MRS. VIOLA van Putten SIMMONDS, A GREAT STORYTELLER WHO TAUGHT ME SO MUCH

For: The strong, resourceful, and resilient residents of the Virgin Islands, US and British, who endured the wrath of a relentless Irma and the ire of a defiant María

EXPLICATORY NOTES

Bamboula dance—West African dance once popular in the Virgin Islands. The word Bamboula is a type of drum.

Big Yard—A popular space where many Virgin Islanders lived during the 1950's and 1960's. A place for storytelling and news, gathering, fellowship.

Bings—This was a young man who in the 1960's frequented several neighborhoods in St. Thomas, U.S. Virgin Islands. Pearson Gardens Housing Project was a regular hang-out. Bings had a most interesting MO: He always carried a small note pad and a pen in his pocket. His robust, infectious laughter brought smiles to the faces of those of us who considered ourselves his friends. As it turned out, he was a superb marble player.

Budhoe—St. Croix, 19th century; the great Moses Gottlieb, General Bordeaux, emancipator, later deported for his so-called "subversive" activities. One of the great Virgin Islands heroes, often buried under the dust of distorted history.

Butty— A naturally gifted storyteller from St. Thomas, Virgin Islands. In the 50's & 60's he kept his audience spellbound with impeccable timing and a perfect.

Coromantees—This is a reference to the Akan people of Ghana, an integral player in U.S.V.I. history, protagonists in 1733 revolt in St, John.

Cow Foot Woman—Part of the lore of the US. Virgin Islands. The claim was that people saw this woman who had the feet of a cow. Unfortunately, no one ever got close enough to converse with her! Yet, everyone claimed her authenticity, and insists that he or she had proof.

Deh Box—According to legend, this suspicious item appeared on the St. Thomas waterfront and no one seemed to know the origin.

Elmot Wilmot Blyden—Born in St. Thomas in 1832, moved to Liberia, founded pan-Africanism, was a diplomat, and educator who was instrumental in changing the world.

Emancipation Proclamation- July 3, 1848, the so-called emancipation of the slaves in the Danish West Indies.

Gade—Danish word for street

Green Face Man—A mythical creation in the Virgin Islands during the 1950's and 1960's. The rumor was that this individual roamed the islands. No one ever provided actual proof of seeing him; of course, claims of sightings were numerous.

Housin'—Pearson Garden Housing Project, a development that opened in 1954 in St. Thomas. It was the first development of its kind on St. Thomas and thus was simply referred to as "Housin."

Hurricanes David and Frederick—Made their entry in 1979 in St. Thomas, Virgin Islands

Hurricane Hugo—-Powerful gale in 1989 that caused extensive damage to St. Croix, and did considerable less to St. Thomas and St. John.

Hurricane Marilyn —1995, US Virgin Islands, a very powerful storm that caused much damage to all our U.S. Virgin Islands

Irma and María—Two vicious storms hitting the Virgin Islands in September of 2017, causing unprecedented damage.

Lucumí—In Cuba this is the word used for "Yoruba."

Mongoose—This animal was imported in our islands to get rid of the snake.

Negerhollands—Virgin Islands Dutch Creole prevalent in the 18th and 19th centuries. It was spoken more in St. Thomas and St. John than on St. Croix. From all historical indications it was morphologically and syntactically *similar* to the Papiamentu spoken in Sint Maarten.

Peter von Scholten—Appointed Governor-General of the Danish West Indies from 1835 to 1848.

Picha—the principal marble used in the marble game.

Quaksa—Excellent marble player, the best of the best.

Queen Breffu—A leader in the 1733 revolt in St. John

Queen Coziah—Leader of the historic Coal Workers Strike on St. Thomas in 1892

Queen Mary—The chief proponent of the anti-Contract Day rebellion in 1878. This is a figure too often submerged in history's revisionist archives.

Sister Esther—An American missionary who gave regular Biblical lessons to children in the various big yards in St. Thomas n the 1950's.

Tampo—A Virgin Islands legend who was known for his strength and good will. He was born in Tortola, British Virgin Islands. But like most residents of the British and U.S. Virgin Islands, he traveled regularly between both the British and U.S. islands. Undoubtedly, he became one of the great mythical creations in all of our Virgin Islands.

Undah deh Bongolo—The site also referred to as *"Deh markit"* in St. Thomas, for more than a century, an important sacred site—of slave trade and sales; the center of culture and St. Thomas' identity.

Victor Cornelins—Born in St. Croix as Victor Cornelius. As a child taken from his island against his will to Denmark and displayed in an amusement park as a "human exhibit."

BINGS DEH QUAKSA

He began to laugh, as he so often did after winning yet another marble game. It was his signature laughter. Strangely enough, the young children would not have been able to recognize his voice if he had ever spoken. But everyone was familiar with his infectious laughter.

– "Why yoh laughin' like dat, Mr.?" asked Wayne, one of the marble players in the midst. But the quiet man, as was his style, did not respond with words:

–"Hee hee, hee," he bellowed, a very unique laughter that always caught everyone's attention.

As was customary, many of his competitors in the marble game would also begin to laugh, almost on cue. Bings came regularly to the playground, this man of no words, but none of the children was able to explain exactly who he was, where he lived on St. Thomas, or how old he was. He was a kind of a mystery man, with origins unknown. It all began one typical sunny Virgin Islands afternoon in the 1950's when a group of boys from the *Pearson Gardens Housing Project* decided to play one of their typical games of marbles. Marble playing was a popular activity, a cherished recreational pastime, not only in that housing development, more commonly referred to as *"Housin,"* but also in every region of the Virgin Islands. To someone unfamiliar with this game, the words and phrases probably may seem strange, as if one were speaking a different language, because the boys were employing such terms as *"linguis," "t(h)ree up," "fat," "bottin' full,"* and *"set."* These were expressions inherently linked to the functioning of

1

the game, and all players understood the particular language necessary to make the competition successful.

Just as Allen told one of the players, "I set heh," through the corner of his eyes he noticed someone that he had never seen before looking very intently at the game. The stranger, watching with a smile, was a thin man probably in his early twenties who was wiping his brow because of the sweat caused by the 90 degrees heat on that mid-summer day in the West Indies. It was a paradoxical demeanor, for the man seemed to be looking away from the players, yet scrutinizing their every move. Because he did not have a handkerchief, or paper towel, the visitor used his open palms to dry his forehead, already dripping with sweat.

— "Who da man is?" a boy nicknamed Crimmo asked.

The boys decided to halt the game because everyone was very curious to know the identity of the man who was roughly10 to 12 years their senior. Other noises could be heard from other areas on the playground where children were riding on a merry-go-round, while others were playing softball. A girl named Lois was skating with her friends, Blue, Janet and a girl nicknamed Tin Tin on the sidewalk that the children had christened "New Road." While about fifty yards away Vernie, Louiche, Toochie, Tiny and other children were playing basketball on a concrete court. But, none of this really mattered to Hector, Allen, Myie, and other excellent marble players who simply wanted to determine the identity of the newcomer who still had not introduced himself. Above all, they wanted to assess his skill as a marble player.

—"Hi, mista," said Tito. "Wa' yoh name?"

—"Yoh wan' toh play wid we?" echoed Sidney a boy from building 11.

—"Hee, hee, hee," laughed the silent man who still would not respond in words.

—"Den watch we play," said Sidney.

—"Yes, mista', maybe yoh cou' learn ah ting' oh two from we," chimed in Ala who along with Snoop had just joined the game.

—"Hee, hee, hee," responded the man in a tone that made it very clear that he was very happy to be in the company of the enthusiastic marble players.

With their new friend watching, the boys continued their game, constantly mixing play with frequent conversations, jokes, discussion of rules, and even arguments. This kind of interaction was very common among these adolescents who saw each other daily and played not only games but also recreational and competitive sports together. It was not at all unusual to have visitors to this area. Many boys and girls from places called *Downstreet, Polybuck, 'Roun' de Fiel', Bay Side, Savan, Garden Street* and *Silva Dolla'* frequently came to the Pearson Gardens location to compete in sports or to simply play with other children. The place was like a magnet for play, frolic, and fun. But all the children that came, no matter from what part of the island they originated, would chat with the boys and girls who resided there. But the stranger with the distinct and frequent laughter was different. Always shoeless, he carried a pencil, or pen in his shirt pocket, along with a small note pad.

—"Mista', why yoh have dem ting in yoh pocket?" asked Buddy, one of the marble players.

—"Yoh wastin' yoh time," said Blakey. "Da' man 'ain gon talk toh we."

—"Maybe he carn' talk," said Errol. "I read about ah man who ah stop' speakin' after ah lot ah years. Deh doctors dem couldn' tell why he wuzin' talkin'. Dey say it wus psychological or sumtin' like dat."

—"Was psycho-wa?" inquired one of the boys. "Wey yoh learn' such a big word?"

—"Oh, Ah see dat word in one ah dem Dell Comic books that Ah len' from Fordy."

During that time period most of the homes on the island did not have television sets; so the children spent a lot of time reading and exchanging comic books.

—"Yoh know," said a fellow named Tony, "maybe he wan' toh geh in deh game."

As Hector turned to the guest to ask if he would be willing to join the game, the boys noticed that he was writing furiously in his little notepad. It almost seemed as though he was anxious to record what was going on.

—"He some kind ah reporta' o sumtin'?" asked Tony's brother, Charles.

—"Maybe he is ah spy," said Dacka who was always playful. "Well, anyway, mista', take dese marbles; we gon leh yoh play wid we."

To everyone's surprise, the quiet man indicated by shaking his head negatively that he did not want to accept anyone's marbles. Instead, he reached into his pants pocket and pulled out a lot of marbles, often referred to as a "*budge*t." His face lit up; there was no doubt that this man who lived in his world of silence was ready to be a part of the world of these young boys, their world of games, of fun. Some kind of alliance was being formed on that hot summer's day.

—"Five up," suggested Blackie.

—"Dat's too much," objected Bayie. "Deh po' man probably carn' play a bit ah marble; we doan' want toh win arl he marbles right away. We ain' wan' him toh feel bad."

But the silent stranger indicated with his five fingers that he was willing to wager five marbles from his small "budget."

—"Hee, hee, hee," he laughed, once more showing his five fingers—long, bony fingers, attached to the rather frail hand of a young man whose life was still a mystery to his future marble competitors.

The best players were alternating victories. Some competitors were even feeling angry or sad because they were losing their marbles. It was not uncommon to have a boy say, "I quit," if he felt that he was not being successful. Or, even worse, one or two boys might yell:

—*"Mama say,… fall in, scratch."*

Typically when the players heard this, they would all run to the marble ring in order to try to retrieve some of the marbles. This was always seen as bad gamesmanship, and sometimes resulted in fisticuffs. Some of the players on the warm summer afternoon were suspecting that the tall outsider would probably try this last minute tactic, if he felt desperate. To many, he had that look of someone who was sneaky and conniving. The truth is that they could not quite figure him out.

—"I doan' trus' 'im," said Ed, a boy from Savan who frequented the Housin' area. "If he start toh lose, he might try toh scratch."

—"No" said Ponto, "He probably even doan know dat we do dat kina ting 'roun' heh sometimes. Let's giv'im ah chance, man."

It was clear that the boys were feeling sorry for the visitor and had already concluded that he was not capable of playing against such able players as they were.

—"Mista', come play wid us," invited one of the boys.

—"Hee, hee, hee," laughed the guest, but this time the laughter sounded somewhat differently, as if he wanted to thank the boys for allowing him to participate in the game.

When it was his turn to play, the new player pointed to his "picha," – his principal marble– and then immediately pointed to Hector's marble, signaling clearly that he was going to try to eliminate Hector from the game. Taking careful aim, the thin marble man let loose his marble, striking that of his competitor, thus achieving his goal. All the boys seemed to be in a state of shock, especially since this feat was accomplished from a distance of almost five feet away. In a marble game this is an amazing accomplishment. However, no one said anything, until Mac bellowed:

—"Man, dat was ah fluke. No one can play dat good. Even Hector never "hit" nobardy from so far." The visiting marble player with the deadly aim, looked at Buddy, this time without a smile, without laughter, and pointed at his marble. With accuracy he also hit that marble some five or six feet away.

—"Whew," said Butty, "he fo' real. He is ah amazin' marble player."

Just then the quiet marble competitor paused to write something in his secret book pad. Was he keeping score? Was he recording the names of the boys that he had eliminated from the game? Was he recording his secret thoughts? Or was he simply a poet, poeticizing his own life? No one could answer the many questions concerning this man of intrigue and mystery, who was writing non-stop in his secret world of the written word.

It did not take long before the ageless, nameless man had filled all of his pockets with the marbles of his competitors. All of the boys present that day were looking at him in awe, caught somewhere between utter confusion, and some embarrassment for having underestimated someone. It was a valuable lesson for the boys from "Housin" who always felt that they could outplay and outmaneuver anyone in any sport or game.

—"Mista', wa' yoh name?"

—"How yoh learn toh play so?"

—"Who teach yoh?

—"Wey yoh from?"

These were some of the rapid-fire questions that the astonished boys were asking, especially after witnessing their best players falling to defeat by the man with no spoken words. The day following the defeat of the best players, everyone became even more curious about the stranger's identity. One boy returned to the site of the marble games with some news.

—"Mey mudda' say dat she know who deh man family is, and dat people call him "Bings," said Eldridge.

—"Bings? Dat's a strange name for a good marble player," laughed his brother Blakey, one of the players who lost most of his marbles.

Shortly after hearing that comment the boys were surprised to see the visitor was again walking toward them.

—"Hi, Bings! Come ova' heh. Yoh want toh play again?" asked another boy.

Before Bings came very close to the group that was preparing to play another game, one of the marble players objected:

—"Ah yoh crazy? Da man win most of our marbles yestaday. Ah like it betta' wen he jus' be watchin', smilin', o' laughin'."

—"We lose ah lot ah marbles, but it was so much fun jus' watchin' him play," said Ed the Savan Fellow, "I neva' know dat somebardy cou' be so good."

—"Hi Bings," said Blackman, "we wan' toh change yoh name."

—"Yeah," echoed Teddy, "we gon call yoh *Bings, Deh Quaksa,* the bes' marble player."

Bings' eyes once again lit up, for even though he spoke no words, he was clearly communicating with the group. He knew that day that he was an integral part of this band of players; he was being accepted and recognized not merely as a good marble player, but was being crowned as the best of the very best.

—"Yoh is ah Quaksa, Bings," shouted Diamon.

—"Hee, hee, hee" laughed Bings the Quaksa with a hearty laughter as he wrote more enthusiastically in his secret book, off limits to his new friends.

All the other boys chimed in with laughter, well aware that Bings would never again be a stranger in the midst. He would always be the Quaksa, the cream of the crop. They looked at him admiringly as he wrote in his private book, and it was now clear that he too was aware of his new status.

—"Hee, hee, hee," the Quaksa laughed as he wrote even faster in his notepad of hidden dreams and well-guarded secrets.

TAMPO AN' DEH BREEZE PUNCH

His reputation preceded him anywhere he went in the British or American Virgin Islands. But as might be expected, that same fame made him a prime target for those who were seeking for themselves popularity and acclaim. The man was Tampo, well known in the entire Virgin Islands as a robust, young, strong fellow, with a penchant for working and a respecter of customs and tradition. Not too many people dared stand up to this modest, gentle, non-aggressive man who sought no individual attention. At the same time, it was not at all unusual for some young man trying to impress friends or a girlfriend to provoke Tampo, in an effort to initiate a fistfight. The gentleman that he was, our hero tried his best to avoid these physical conflicts. Ironically, it was his desire for peace that created many more challenges for him, since many of his competitors interpreted his peaceful actions as cowardice. Those who knew him, though, also realized that he took every effort to avert fisticuffs. His walking was legendary, and it was general knowledge that he thought nothing of walking from Road Town to West End, a distance of some 10-12 miles. His walking exploits were well chronicled and elaborated in the oral annals of Virgin Islands lore. One bright morning he decided to take a stroll of several miles. It was an amazingly beautiful day on the island of Tortola noted for its graceful hills, such as Sage, and others. The priceless view looking down onto Cane Garden Bay from various strategic points called attention to the fact that this island is indeed a paradise, with its many Edens.

Tampo never tired of these inimitable views that his island offered him daily. He loved climbing the hills and looking down on what is clearly a divine work of art. It was there that he first met the persistently irritating man, himself an unabashed admirer of his island's mountains chains and matchless beaches. Their fate became intertwined that day when the man spotted Tampo walking briskly in Long Bay's majestically scenic route.

—"Hi, you mus' be Tampo," shouted the arrogant sounding man, already insulting Tampo with his total disregard for island manners. "Ah been hearin' 'bout how yoh so strong, an' how yoh cou' beat anybardy in ah fight. But toh meh yoh notin' but ah fraud."

—"Listen, partna'," responded Tampo already bored because he had been through such situations often enough, and was therefore immediately aware of the man's intention. "Ah 'ain have no interes' in fightin' nobardy. We doan have toh prove notin'. Mos' ah all, Ah doan' have toh prove mey' manhood. Ah simply wish toh be lef' alone. We 'ain rivals; meh ain yoh enemy an' yoh ain mey enemy. Ah even ain' know yoh."

—"Dat is because you is ah coward," offered the man, later identified as Gully. Your fame is base' on deh fact dat yoh dus intimidate weaklings, but I different. You ain as strong as deh people dem say. Yoh so-call' strenk is all ah joke, ah untrut, maybe ah scheme devise' by you yohself, toh falsely define who yoh tink yoh is, toh seek fame deh quick way."

None of what Gully was saying had any ring of truth to it; in fact, everyone knew that Tampo was the complete opposite of what this inciter was trying to portray. They too had heard all it all before. But not only was he a mild mannered individual, but he was also an outgoing, friendly, church-going man who loved nothing better than associating with his fellow and sister citizens of Tortola. He was also revered on other islands. Everyone knew that he was no troublemaker.

—"Tink wa' yoh want," said Tampo to the man who was by now flexing his muscles in a typical attempt to intimidate him. "Now le' meh continue on mey way."

It was true that Gully had some limited fame. A man of great style and charm, he was an ostentatious dresser whose penchant for public adulation was known throughout the land. Someone had tipped Gully off to the fact that Tampo was headed to West End to do his daily swim. Tampo's swimming routine, combined with his regular hard work as a producer and transporter of coal, had made him a well-conditioned man. It was said that he carried several bags of coals on his head while holding one big bag in each hand. His legend was already carved out in its special place in Virgin Islands oral lore. This demonstration of strength, however, did not deter Gully, who had promised all his friends that this was going to be the day that he humiliated Tampo. In the process he would debunk once and for all the "so-call' myt' ah dis Tampo fella," as he was fond of saying. The thought crossed Gully's mind: *If Ah cou' destroy Tampo in ah public match, Ah would be considered deh stronges' man truout all ah deh Virgin Islands, British and American."*

–"Tampo!" he screamed, in part to impress his future rival with his robust voice. "Ah challenge you toh ah fight ah three rounds to prove once and for all who is deh stronges' in dese parts. Ah fast, ah strong; yoh would not las' too long 'genz' me."

–"Please Gully, le' meh alone. Ah 'ain have no grudge 'genz' you or nobardy else. An' if Ah did, Ah doan' believe in resolvin' conflicts wid arguments an' fights. Not tru' no violence. No, Mr. Gully, Ah doan' want toh lowa' meyself toh dat level ah deh animals dem."

No sooner had Tampo spoken his words that a throng of people gathered, seemingly from nowhere. But the sense was that Gully had informed many of friends and supporters of his intentions, so that they could be witnesses to his exploits, his defeat of the strongest Virgin Islander. It was also clearly a set-up. Gully wanted to confront Tampo and have witnesses who would say that Tampo seemed scared, afraid of the possibility that Gully's legend would eventually replace his as the most fearsome man. The simple truth was that our protagonist only wanted peace.

–"Wat' is dis'? Tampo turnin' soft?" one of Gully's backers asked of no one in particular.

–"Maybe wa' we been hearin' 'bout 'im is all lies," laughed another.

Meanwhile, amidst it all, Tampo maintained his quiet demeanor, mumbling too himself, "Me 'ain wan' no trouble wid dis man, yoh know."

But encouraged by the chanting crowd and its constant disparagement of Tampo, Gully became more convinced than ever that Tampo was afraid of him. Even more importantly, Gully thought, "Tampo is 'fraid 'because he know dat ah gon defeat 'im. Above all, Gully felt disrespected; he felt that Tampo belittled him when he spoke of not wanting "toh lowa meyself toh dat level ah deh animals dem." How dare this man refer to him in the same breath with the animals! Gully felt that those were fighting words. Only true gladiators would be able to read such subtle signals, he reasoned.

–"Come on Mista strong fella; live up toh yoh big name, yoh fakey reputation; yoh so coward, Ah say again, COWARD!" taunted Gully, still encouraged by Tampo's reluctance to engage in battle.

There was something particularly derisive in those remarks that really struck at the heart of Tampo's pride. Yet, he did everything to resist Gully's enticement; but when he could no longer defend himself verbally he finally began to see Gully as another of his misguided rivals. Tampo could withstand almost anything, but the idea of being a coward always rubbed him the wrong way. He was a man who withstood a lot of heckling and challenges over his many years, but the derision of his character at some point always forced him to defend his honor and restore his sense of dignity.

–"Set ah time an' place, man. We cou' meet and settle dis situation, whatever it is," responded Tampo rather defiantly.

Gully now anxious, could hardly wait to demonstrate to the naysayers that he rightfully deserved the title as: "Stronges' Virgin Islander." Or so he thought. "Saturday at nine in the marnin' in West End," were Gully's final words as he exhibited through his bravado more style than substance.

It could very well be that deep down Gully was truly fearful, especially considering the fact that Tampo had been known to stop horses, donkeys, and mules in their tracks. It was rumored that one unfortunate mule learned a valuable lesson as he kicked Tampo one day, only to be slapped by the man, who it was said had callous hands. The mule, according to witnesses, ran scared and in pain from West End to Long Look, a long distance even for a mule. It was agreed upon that on that day the poor mule would have outrun any champion horse. It might very well be that Gully was secretly concerned about the fact that Tampo had been seen lifting cinder blocks, just for fun, it was said. But, too late, Gully had committed himself, and, even more telling, he had done so in front of hundreds of witnesses, friends and foes alike. False pride suddenly became his number one enemy.

But Tampo himself harbored a deep secret— he did not really want to fight Gully, not that he was afraid of his flashy rival. On the contrary, it was that Tampo was a sensitive man whose main mission was to follow the Biblical edict "to do good unto others," to relate well with his neighbors, to lend a helping hand wherever and whenever possible. His altruism knew no limits. It was not at all rare to see him working for free in a neighbor's coal pit, or in that of a stranger whom he volunteered to help. Above all, Tampo was a good man, a good human being, who was a victim of his own physical prowess and reputation. Throughout all of Gully's taunting and teasing, Tampo's main objective was to keep his pride and his dignity intact. But deep down, he was hoping that a miracle would occur, that his newly formed "enemy," would somehow come to his senses, realizing the folly of his ways. Tampo began to hope that maybe, just maybe, this fellow islander, Gully, would somehow reflect on Tampo's history, how it is that he had been able to deter many antagonists long before Gully. Many much stronger, much quicker, much bigger than Gully. Many men who had tried to define their manhood or regain their sense of *machismo* by engaging Tampo. All had failed miserably!

Unfortunately for Gully, the idea of "cowardice" kept spinning in Tampo's head. Gully's "rival" must act. His pride and dignity were at stake.

"You know," thought Tampo on that fateful day, "Ah really doan want toh hut dis man. Ah jus' wan' toh ketch he one fis', toh teach he ah simple lesson. Ah know dat wen dat happen he will neva' again bodda me; jus' one time.... jus' one time; Ah wan' toh ketch he one!"

By then the word had already spread rapidly throughout all the Virgin Islands; people were traveling, even in row boats from St. Thomas, St, John, and St. Croix, Virgin Gorda, Josh Van Dyke, and Anegada to Tortola to see this face off, *"Deh fight ah deh year,"* many had said, maybe with some exaggeration. But it was truly going to be a big event, pitting two men of contrasting styles, will, and principles.

–"Did Tampo finally meet his match? Is this man Gully really that good a fighter? Or is he just one of those people who always talk their way to victory?" These were some of the typical questions that were being heard around the islands. The public was soon to find out the answers.

At five o'clock Saturday morning bright and early the impatient Gully awoke and immediately began to adorn himself in his usual flamboyant manner- - his two-tone shoes, beautiful cream pants, and a tight black T-shirt that revealed his athletic built. It was a sunny day on magnificent Tortola; the sea gulls, circled around as if they too had been informed of the big confrontation, and they wanted to secure their vantage point in the air. The people who were waiting to catch their boats to other islands postponed their trips. In fact, it was later learned that the captains of two ferries canceled the morning trips to afford everyone the chance to see the spectacle. Some at the time felt that it was bigger than August Monday celebrations, St. Croix's or St. Thomas' Carnival, or St. John's Festival. At least, in Gully's mind, there was no question as to which event was the most important one!

When Gully finally showed up at West End, his shoes glittering in the beautiful Tortola sun, he was not even sweating, having arrived on a mule named *"Donno Betta'"* owned by a nice gentleman, Mr. Wally, from Carrot Bay. His hair was well combed, his T-shirt artfully tucked in, and his new red socks were consistent with his ostentatious flare. Gully was ready for the battle! When the crowd saw him, they were impressed with his attitude, the confidence that he seemed to be exuding, the way he was interacting with the crowd, his prognostication. This was typical Gully. Then all of a sudden heads began to turn, when in the distance the crowd saw a figure walking rapidly in the direction where the event was slated to begin. The individual wore no shoes, was moving briskly, and had a bag of coal on his head and two in his hands. As it turned out, Tampo had just walked 10 miles. He had promised three families in West End that he would drop off bags of coal for them so that they could bake that customary delicious bread in those well-constructed outdoor ovens regularly seen on Tortola. Tampo was a man of his word, a man of honor.

As he neared the crowd, no shoes, no shirt, he was heard mumbling to himself: *"Ah jus' wan' toh ketch he one."* The bewildered crowd began to think that maybe Tampo was hallucinating. His comment seemed far too disconnected.

"Yoh tired Tampo?" someone shouted from the dense throng.

—"No, man. Dat ten mile walk was jus' toh warm meh up ah 'lil bit. Ah done mad wid dis man Gully for causin' meh toh miss doing mey work this marnin'. Ah still have 10 bags ah coal toh deliver. Wen Ah promise people sometin' Ah like toh do it. Ah doan like toh fool people."

—"Yoh wan' toh borrow mey mule toh make yoh delivery, Tampo?" asked another spectator.

—"No sir," retorted Tampo. "Dem duz move much too slow fo' me. Ah jus' wan' toh hit dis Gully fella one time, den Ah gon be free toh finish mey daily task dem. *Ah jus' wan' toh ketch he one!*"

Meanwhile Gully was confused, not quite knowing whether to admire or fear this unusually energetic man. "Maybe he don' tired, winded from all dat liftin' and larng distance walkin'. Dis is my day toh make Virgin Islands history. Toh become ah Virgin Islands legen'," Gully's imagination and hopeful thinking were dominating his thoughts.

Just then someone gave the signal and the fisticuffs officially began. In round one, Gully began dancing, and weaving, throwing jabs and feinting. One or two jabs vaguely touched the sturdy chin of this robust man, Tampo. The latter without much reaction kept moving forward, slowly, deliberately, mumbling once again: *"Ah jus' wan toh ketch he one,"* was our hero's constant refrain.

The crowd, impressed by Gully's movement and bravado started to question whether or not Tampo's days of glory had passed indeed. Was he just living off of his reputation? Is this the end of the legend of Tampo? Tampo a Has Been? Some even started to question openly.

Animated and encouraged, Tampo's rival threw more hooks and uppercuts than ever and more of them began to connect the face and stomach of Tampo, however, the barefoot warrior did not flinch. The punches did not feel more than an insignificant tickle to him.

"Ah defeatin' the great Tampo," bristled Gully with enthusiasm and premature celebration, as the first round came to an uneventful end.

"*Ah jus' wan' toh ketch he one,*" whispered Tampo to no one in particular at the start of round two. Still moving forward, and somewhat bored by the commotion and Gully's antics, he continued his conversation with himself, largely ignoring those around him: "*Mey boy, Ah jus' wan toh ketch he one,*" he repeated as the fight neared the end of the second round.

It was just then that Gully moved closer, incorrectly sensing that he was intimidating his rival, and that he was on his way to victory and new found reputation, certain that Tampo's demise was inevitable. Two more jabs by the dancing, prancing, ostentatious and over-confident Gully.

"*Ah jus' wan toh ketch he on*e," repeated Tampo, only slightly exasperated and frustrated by Gully's evasiveness, and not at all fearful of the loquacious rambler's powder puff punches.

It was then that Tampo saw an opening. Gully had thrown his patented uppercut, missed, and left his whole body exposed and unprotected. According to those present, Tampo threw a most vicious right cross, a punch so hard that those around said they felt the vibration. In fact, some people in Carrot Bay, Long Bay, and Cane Garden Bay mentioned that it felt as if the earth were shaking. The time that they gave actually coincided with the moment that Tampo unleashed what is believed to be the most potent punch in Virgin Islands pugilistic history. People in St. Croix, St. John, Virgin Gorda, Anegada, Josh Van Dyke and St. Thomas also reported feeling something shaking; like a "rumblin' quake," said many of the residents. Some even in Nevis and St. Kitts spoke of a quiver in the earth, even though it was never proven if this was a result of Tampo's forceful punch.

The punch, thrown with evil intention, missed its mark. Unfortunately for Gully, however, the force of the missed punch was so devastating that he felt a sharp pain in his ribs, broken by the resulting breeze that according to witnesses came accompanied by a sound of gale winds, like the gales of the 1950's. Gully, in obvious discomfort, conceded, hanging his head in shame, in utter disgrace.

By that time the crowd was repeatedly chanting Tampo's name. He had once again lived up to his reputation. The main thing on the victor's mind now was delivering the coal that he had promised. But, as for his rival Gully, he jumped on the first mule that he saw and headed home. Our epic hero, still bored and unimpressed by the noise, celebration, and adulation, kept whispering to himself, noticeably disappointed and annoyed:

"Bai, yoh know, Ah still ain' ketch he one!"

THE WOMAN WHO BAKED AND
THE DOG WHO BARKED

It was not at all unusual to walk by the little wood house where she lived as early as five in the morning and see her outside fanning the flames of her coal pot. At this early hour, she and Gravy, a slow walking, quiet mangy mutt would be the only beings moving around in her yard. Anyone who walked by knew without doubt that Miss Annie was already mixing her ingredients, and preparing her bread and pastries to sell that day. People came from various points of the island to make sure that the well-known baker would reserve their orders.

—"Make sure yoh save ah coc'nut bread fo' me," a voice urged from the distance.

—"Doan worry, James," responded Miss Annie. "Ah ain' forget."

—"I wan' 5 rolls an' two sal'fish cake," a woman's voice rang out.

—"Now Miss Berta; yoh well know dat in 10 years ah neva' fail toh deliva' yoh requests dem," said Miss Annie.

—"Sure," said Miss Berta laughing, "Ah jus' wan' toh make sure dat' yoh keep yoh perfec' record. Maybe Gravy cou' help you."

—"Oh no, mey chile," said Miss Annie, "dis is the lazies' darg in Savan. But, Ah must admit, 'is good toh have he company while Ah wok this early in the marnin'."

The baker and the customers did not see each other as they spoke, but both James and Miss Berta knew that Miss Annie would always be outside baking. She had established a reputation as a skillful, reliable baker who treated her customers with the utmost respect, and knew all their names. In turn, she was cherished and respected by all. She was a tall dignified woman, between forty and forty-five years old who operated her bakery from her home. People rushed to her house to buy rolls that were tastier that any roll coming from the well-established bakeries around town. Very often, if one did not go there very early, by mid-morning the bread was all sold out, bought by customers who waited patiently to sink their teeth in Miss Annie's very delicious culinary products.

Miss Annie lived in a Big Yard, a kind of arrangement that brought various families together as a community. In the middle of the yard was a well used by everyone to fetch water. The house in which she lived with her four children was not very large. It was a typical structure, with no inside kitchen, and the one huge bedroom was divided in two or more sections by a partition or partitions, made of wood, or at times a curtain would serve as divider. Without exception there were always one or two dogs lying lazily on the dusty ground of the Big Yard. In the Yard that Miss Annie called her home, one of the dogs would always be Gravy, a small insignificant looking canine that barely opened his eyes, except when it was time to eat. Even heavy rains and gale winds could not move him from his favorite spot, in a corner a few feet away from Miss Annie's cooking operation. Gravy was so lazy that the people who lived in the Big Yard always joked that there was at least a second between his "*Bow*" and his "*Wow.*" One neighbor joked: "Gravy, yoh is deh perfec' watch darg. If anybardy try toh steal Miss Annie tasty products, Ah guess yoh gon jus' watch dem."

-"Ha, Ha, Ha" laughed everyone in the Big Yard.

—"Gravy, Ah wish that you wus able toh really help me, instead ah jus' lyin' de wid yoh eyes dem half-close, yoh lazy self," Miss Annie complained only half jokingly.

The dog barely opened one of his eyes as Miss Annie spoke, as if he understood what she was saying, but was not too impressed. He took comfort in the fact that because nothing was expected of him, he could live the lofty life as "king canine" of The Big Yard.

It was time to wake up the children.

—"Eveybardy wake up! 'Is already 5:00," insisted Miss Annie as she woke them up one by one.

One of the reasons that Miss Annie was so successful was the fact that every child was a part of her business operation. For example, the younger children Sonny and Guirlie were responsible for gathering the flour, sugar, and grated coconut and putting them in one location so that their mother would have easy access to them. The older children, Lou and Lorna, were responsible for bringing water from the well. In the Big Yard there were several buckets with ropes tied to them, and Lou and Lorna were able to use them to bring the water to the area where Miss Annie would be working on any given morning.

This particular early Saturday morning the children fulfilled their responsibilities very quickly, placing the rolls, patés, johnny cakes and other niceties on the table that Miss Annie used to organize her goods. Every Saturday Mr. Davis, Miss Annie's husband, took some of the goods to the Market to be sold at a venerable site called "Deh Bongolo." At this place one could buy fresh fruits, vegetables, fish, and bread, and various types of candy. On this bright Virgin Islands day, Mr. Davis gathered numerous baskets that he used to transport the items to the market. The baskets were regularly kept hanging in the ceiling of the house, an island tradition that dated back many years.

—"Annie, come quick," shouted Mr. Davis suddenly in a frantic voice. "Ah doan see deh bake goods dem."

Because her husband was always playing pranks, Miss Annie did not pay him much attention, but instead responded:

—"Alfred, stop wastin' people time. Geh serious. Yoh know dat deh people go toh deh Bongolo very early. Yoh gon make meh lose some ah mey customers."

But, unfortunately, Mr. Davis was not joking. Miss Annie was shocked as she noticed that the table that she customarily used was bare. Something strange had happened, and no one was able to explain it. "All mey effort, and dat ah mey family garn toh waste," she lamented. More importantly, however, was the fact that customers would be very disappointed because they always looked forward to savoring Miss Annie's products. It was above all a question of integrity, honor, and respect. She could not stand the thought of ruining her good name. "A reputation is arl yoh geh in dis worl'," she said to herself in a kind of self-analysis and introspection.

The residents of the Yard assured Miss Annie that they did not see any stranger entering or leaving the Yard. It was a mystery that not even Sherlock Holmes could solve. Because there were no residential telephones during this period in the 1950's in the Virgin Islands, Mr. Davis decided to walk to Deh Bongolo to inform Miss Annie's customers that unfortunately their favorite breads and cakes would not be available on that day.

As he was approaching the entrance to the Big Yard, he heard a very robust and constant

—**"BOW WOW BOW WOW!"**

It was an unfamiliar sound in that communal Yard of general peace, quiet, and harmony.

—"Ah wonda' wa' darg makin' dat crazy noise so early in deh marnin'," Mr. Davis thought to himself. "It geh toh be ah darg from anodda' Yard, some ferocious animal."

As he got closer and closer to the entrance the sound became louder and more furious.

—**"BOW WOW. BOW WOW BOW WOW. BOW WOW."**

Mr. Davis followed the sound and then heard the voice of someone pleading:

"Please geh' dat vicious darg away from me. Ah beg yoh doan le' 'im harm me."

It was the voice of a desperate man, who was trapped in a corner pleading for the loud barking dog to let him go. Next to the man were several baskets filled with Miss Annie's products.

—"See deh baskets dem de. Jus' take dis attack darg away from meh," the frantic man begged Mr. Davis before the latter had even gotten to where the stranger was crouched.

—"Wa' darg dat is?" asked Mr. Davis, not at all familiar with such aggressive barking.

As he got closer Mr. Davis shouted in astonishment:

—"Gravy? Ah carn' believe dis!! Gravy, dat carn be you makin' arl dat noise in deh place. Yoh save' deh day, Gravy. Yoh save our day!"

By this time the rest of the family and other residents of the Big Yard had gathered around and were admiring and applauding the new hero, Gravy, the newly crowned "**WATCH DOG OF DEH YARD**."

"Thanks toh you, Gravy, mey customers dem gon be happy dis marnin'," praised Miss Annie the baker.

"**Bow…..Wow**," replied Gravy very assertively, as he returned to his favorite spot next to Miss Annie's coal pot, with one eye barely opened, and hardly enjoying his new status as hero of the Big Yard.

THE UNLIKELY ALLIANCE: GUANA AN' DEM

No one could recall when the conflict between Mongoose and the Guana began. It was only known that there was a long history of bitterness, anger, and resentment. The truth is that the two did not know each at all, only occasionally getting a glimpse of one another as they made their way through the bush and thicket in very dense areas in Grove Place, Bethlehem, and Kings Hill, St. Croix in the United States, Virgin Islands. Mongoose felt convinced that Guana was harboring strong feelings of jealousy because of the important role that the former has played with regard to the control of the snake population.

—"Wat ah pity!" Mongoose lamented to a friend, "obviously the green-eye monsta don take control of 'Guana, and he can neva' appreciate deh fact dat our role is ah unique one in dese islands."

—"Yoh right," responded the friend, also a member of the Mongoose family. Wedder yoh go toh La Vallee, Bethlehem, or Kings Hill it is arl deh same. We receive respect fo' our importance."

—"Guana need toh seek he own legacy," continued Mongoose, now bolstered and encouraged by his friend who was equally adamant about Guana's inferiority as a species of the animal kingdom.

The conversation took place many years ago close to Centerline Road (now called the Queen Mary Highway) when Mongoose and his friend observed Guana trying to cross the street on a blisteringly, hot St. Croix day when cars heading east seemed to be flying. Mongoose's friend was struck by the iguana's bright green color and had remarked that under the bright sun the color seemed unusually unnatural. The friend had suggested to Mongoose that there was something very unreal, perhaps even false about that color.

—"I wou' not be surprise' if dem guanas have some kind ah hidden factory wey dey duz manufacture dat color. Nothin' cou' look dat bright and pretty widout bein' fabricated," the friend said to Mongoose, not at all concerned as to whether or not Guana was overhearing the conversation.

—"Ah don tell yoh aready dat he bright green color is connected toh he jealously. Anoda' ting; watch 'im good," Mongoose had urged that day, "tain have no logical reason why he carn' cross deh street. Ah know dat deh cars dem movin' fas', but he geh enough time toh cross widout any problem. Dem guanas fast! Plus, Centerline Road 'ain a mile in wit'."

—"It only have one obvious explanashun," the friend continued, looking steadfastly at Guana. "It is clear that he ain really want toh cross deh road."

—"Wa yoh mean by dat?" asked Mongoose, feigning confusion and puzzlement.

—"We know he type. He only aim is toh stan' de so dat deh passin' motorists dem cou' talk 'bout he so-called pretty color. Ah read ah editorial in the _**Iguana Chronicle,**_ dey principal newspaper, in which dey praise deyself fo' bein', lemme quote dey own words, '_ah conversashun piece_' fo' deh people from La Vallee, Whim, Federiksted and odda places."

—"Exactly wa' Ah wus tinkin'," added Mongoose elated because his friend was supporting the theory that he has had for so many years. "Dey believe dey prettier dan we, an'..."

"An' yoh cou see dat attitude in dey arrogant walk," interrupted the friend. "Dey walk like dey betta' dan deh res' ah we; it is ah vain walk, typical of ah conceited animal. But yoh know, 'tain all ah dem so pretty. Mo' an' mo' Ah duz see dem funny lookin' brown ones, dat color doan glitta' in deh sun!"

"Ha ha," the two friends laughed in unison.

It was at that point that Guana looked in the direction of the two who were discussing him. He was not at all shocked by the comments that he had overheard, probably because he had his own strong negative feelings about Mongoose. Instead of responding to what he had heard he decided that he would spite the two detractors if he did not cross the street, even if the opportunity presented itself. As he looked east and west on Centerline Road, he observed with glee that there was not a car in sight.

—"Look at how he gon show off he arrogant waddle," shouted Mongoose now very much aware that the iguana had overheard the conversation. To Mongoose and his friend's surprise, however, Guana turned around and started walking back into the bushes. As he walked he recited a popular poem known by all iguanas. And he did so in a loud, pronounced voice so that his two rivals could hear every word. "Fo' sure, dis poem will annoy dem," he mused. Then in the most spirited tradition of the great bards bellowed:

> *Useless Mongoose, wat' ah shame! Yoh lost yoh purpose*
> *Yoh dull color is borin' toh each and every one ah us*
> *Stop walkin' around Cruz' praisin' yohself, fo' heaven's sake*
> *Jus' because years ago dey bring yoh heh toh control deh snake*
> *Now we hea' how yoh like toh chase afta deh po', lil' innocent fowl,*
> *But yoh such ah coward dat yoh duz run if you hea' ah darg growl*
> *Yoh jealous ah Guana because Ah duz carry meyself wid so much class,*
> *But yoh so scared of everyting; yoh duz run if yoh hea' ah ca' pass.*

More insulted than enraged, Mongoose and his friend approached Guana to force him to retract his derogatory comments. How in the world could the editors approve such a vindictive representation without having any evidence? Mongoose was at a lost. He knew that Guana hated him, but he was not aware of the depth of this hate.

—"Yoh need toh show meh some respect," shouted Mongoose. "In fact, Ah demand that yoh respect meh an' mey friend, and dat yoh refrain from recitin' such negative tings 'bout meh an' mey fellow and sister mongoose dem. Yoh ain know ah ting 'bout we. Yoh only goin' by wa' yoh hea' deh guana people dem falsely say."

Guana's response was quite a shock to his rival:

—"Ah only speak wa' Ah know toh be deh trut," shouted back Guana. "Doan blame me. Ah wus'n deh one toh write dem verses ah deh poem. Lemme tell yoh sometin' else. Last week Ah went toh visit some relatives who live close toh the sea out de in beautiful La Vallee. On mey way ova' de Ah happen' toh walk by one ah yoh mongoose schools. Dese verses dat Ah jus' recite' come from verses Ah hea' deh young ones recitin' in dey Mongoose Poetry class. Dey come from yoh own mongoose culture! Doan blame me…..."

—"Fus' of all," chimed in Mongoose's friend, trying to figure out how to respond to such surprising news, "we ain' 'fraid ah notin'. Sure, 'tis true dat we duz run ah lot….but…"

"Yoh duz run ah lot 'cause yoh scared ah everyting; yoh is ah scairdy ciat," interrupted Guana, now all charged up and ready for a verbal battle. "Ah carn' imagine how you use' toh kill snakes. Ah tink dat is ah myt', sometin' make up by yoh elders dem toh give yoh false pride an' fake glory."

—"Wa' you eva' done?" countered Mongoose, "except walk around tryin' toh look pretty, an' even dat Ah must tell yoh, yoh doan do too good."

—"Say wa' yoh wan', but Ah have mey pride. An' Ah 'ain no coward like you. Yoh duz see meh runnin' 'roun' like ah headless chicken wen Ah see ah human bein'? Ah ain 'fraid ah dem; dey only full ah chat. In fact dey jus' like ah you mongoose. Yoh duz see meh runnin' like Ah 'ain know wey pah ah goin'? Ah duz take mey time walkin' dis islun from bush toh bush wid mey guana family, proud ah who we is…."

—"Guana, you ain geh no history. Tell meh yoh Iguana History. Who bring ah you heh an' why? Yoh ain have no legacy, Guana. Yoh life, yoh history, yoh genealogy, all borin'."

—"Maybe" retorted Guana, "but I wasn' imported."

It is just then that the conversation became even more heated. Both Guana and Mongoose were viciously attacking each other verbally, each commenting on the other's looks, and lack of value. It was a remarkable argument since the two never really knew each other, except for brief sightings, or from what each had read about the other in the other's encyclopedia. The situation became so volatile that Mongoose's friend shouted to both of them: "I garn, leavin' ah you two wid ah yoh foolishness."

—"Ah neva' in mey life see ah animal so ugly," continued Guana, ignoring the friend and looking directly at Mongoose's face. "Yoh look like some kind ah distorted rodent."

—"If yoh wan' toh geh personal," responded Mongoose, "yoh walk is absolutely annoyin' toh everyone. Ah dus see deh exaggerated importance in deh way yoh move. Even deh little ones now walk like you. It is shameful; in fact, it is downright disgraceful. Ah would hate toh be you."

—"I ain wan' toh be you, neidda," retorted Guana. "Yoh borin', cowardly, an' nobardy admire yoh. We laugh at your claim of importance, yoh so-call' contribution toh Virgin Islands society, at yoh so-call' popularity in St. Croix…."

—"Stop right de," shouted out Mongoose angrily. "Let me put it in "good" an' respected Mongoose diction:

"I am well-known, quite admired, and thoroughly loved in St. Croix, St. John, St. Thomas, the British Virgin Islands, in fact in all the islands of the West Indies, for your information. What I have accomplished against the snake population is common knowledge in these islands. I am clearly respected for this."

What was most remarkable was that the two kept a safe distance from each other, just screaming their defamatory insults from a secured space. They continued trading insults not at all aware of the bulldozer that was busy cutting away the nearby thicket, in close proximity to the site of the argument. The fact was that the extremely loud and boisterous verbal sparring was drowning out the sound of the machine's engine. Oblivious to this activity, the two "enemies" continued their mudslinging while the bulldozer remained dedicated to the task, unaware of the disagreement taking place in the underworld of the thicket off Centerline Road.

—"I 'ain' gon wase no mo' time wid you," Guana assured his nemesis. "I gon jus' return toh mey home."

—"The feelin' mutual, Mr. Guana," responded Mongoose rather sarcastically, "Yoh is ah t(h)reat toh mey species. I too will now return toh mey home, toh be wid mey family. Ah tired tarkin' toh yoh."

Meanwhile the sound of the bulldozer was becoming more and more ominous.

Both animals turned to leave, and moving in opposite directions they could clearly hear the cacophonic sound of the bulldozer fixated on its mission of destruction.

Both animals glanced back at each other, and for the first time each noticed the barren fields lying ahead of his adversary. There was no doubt that both were now aware that something tragic had occurred. Turning around, each walked toward the other until they came face to face, for the first time in recorded history. No anger, no animosity, because both Guana and Mongoose realized that there was no home to which they could return. No families waiting for them. This mutual understanding was promoting a move toward conciliation.

—"Ah wonda' wa' wou' ah happen' if instead ah arguin' wid you Ah had left toh see wa' wus goin' on in mey bush," Guana said to Mongoose as if speaking to a new found friend.

—"Ah wus tinkin' deh same ting," said Mongoose with a similar demeanor.

For the first time the two were "truly" speaking to each other; the tone of their verbal exchange was different, as if they finally became aware that none was really the threat to the other, as they had wrongfully perceived. The two species were communicating for the first time in documented animal history.

—"I tink dat we need each odda'," Mongoose confessed.

—"I ain 'shame' toh admit dat," Guana responded.

Then together they walked away from the scene wondering where they would live, but discussing the problem with each other, while the bulldozer with its ever-increasing noise continued its destruction of the thickets, not at all impressed by the fact that it had forged a new lasting relationship in the Virgin Islands.

FININ' DEH COWFOOT WOMAN

The adults on the island did not want to believe the children of the small elementary school who kept insisting that they had seen her emerging from some thick kasha bush in the Sugar Estate area. Some of the older children who were not overly paralyzed with fear managed to move close to her, close enough to observe her feet:

"Dem doan look like human foot," whispered one third-grader, Debra as she sprinted toward her classroom to be in the secured presence of her teacher. The teachers at this school had the reputation of excellence, and they always assured the safety of their students. On such a sunny early June day the children would normally flock to the playground to frolic. They would devise games, some passed on to them by their parents, such as "Stealin' deh Bacon" or "Red Light, Green Light," and they would play others of their own generation. Recess time was truly a time of relaxation and fun. But on this day students kept close to their teachers, and in general were maintaining their distance from the normally lively playground. The teachers could not figure out what the problem was, thinking perhaps it was the blazing heat that day.

"Someone or sometin' in dem bushes ova' de close toh the racetrack," Debra confided in one of her teachers.

By this time the students were becoming more and more anxious because many of them had seen for themselves the woman with the unusual feet. They had seen for themselves Deh Cowfoot Woman as she stepped out of the thicket close to the school.

A short time after she had been seen close to the school, Cowfoot walked through other areas on St. Thomas without rest, as a kind of sightseer and observer of Virgin Islands culture. People as far as Bordeaux in the island's West end had sighted her, while others in the area close to Red Hook had seen her in the bushes adjacent to the dock's parking lot. In fact, one young girl, Delaun, had informed the local papers that she saw a strange figure with cow's feet in the Bordeaux area. Her sisters confirmed this. However, people in Smith Bay, Mandahl, Polyberg, Bovoni, and even Garden Street had laughed at the idea of a woman with a cow's feet, because no one there had seen her.

–"Anodda' untrut'," said one man who in an earlier discussion had dismissed the idea of obeah, the existence of the Green Face Man, and the Box. "Ah know dat dese tings doan exist. Dey ain real atarl. " The man was espousing his unabashed rejection of Virgin Islands culture and tradition. To some he seemed to be a chief violator of the codes of cultural ethics. No West Indian ever stays silent in the face of such a challenge.

-–"How do you know dat?" asked another contentious man. "Everyone in dese islands know at leas' one obeah man or woman, many ah dem is our neighbors. As far as deh Green Face Man and the Box is concern, Ah cou' tell you dat Ah don see both ah dem mo' dan once. Mey father was one ah dem police officers in constant search of Green Face, so no one cou' convince meh oddawise. Dat is deh reason that Ah have no doubt about deh Cowfoot Woman. I meyself see ha' many times in Cruz Bay sittin' on deh dock. Ah believe wa' dem chiren in dat school sayin'."

In fact, some residents reported seeing her in the southeastern part of St. John, close to Coral Bay.

In fact, some people claimed to have seen her sitting on the waterfront with her bovine feet hanging over the water. Things began to change one early Saturday morning as people were preparing to go to the Market Square. The island's tradition dictated that vendors took the wares to the market in the early hours of the morning. They would secure their positions early "undah Deh Bongalo'." Customers came to buy mangos, tea leaves, sugar apples, limes, and many other local fruits, meat, fish, or vegetables. It was that morning that one of the Market Square vendors from the Harmony area spotted a medium size figure stepping out of the bushes. At first the vendor, lately identified as Miss Marilyn Tambi, thought that perhaps someone had built a small shed in the bushes and was simply getting ready to go to the market. But on closer examination it became evident that the figure was not totally human. Miss Marilyn, once owner herself of several cows, told friends that she would recognize a cow's feet anywhere:

"Her foot dem look very much like Mebela, ah cow that Ah ha' own fo' many years befo' she dead in 1960 or so. Even deh way dat she duz walk remin' meh ah Mebela, mey faitful cow."

Because she was very uncertain as to what the Cowfoot woman would, or could do to her, Miss Marilyn hid behind a plum tree that had an unusually thick trunk to obscure her image. She spied the Cowfoot Woman as she headed in the direction toward Cassie Hill. "Wey she goin'?" thought Miss Marilyn Tambi to herself.

Not surprisingly, as Cowfoot walked, there was a very noticeable pounding sound, resulting from her contact with the ground. At some points she would begin to gallop, somewhat like a horse, practicing for an upcoming race. With Miss Marilyn maintaining a safe distance, she saw the Cowfoot woman, running in and out of the thick brush along the way to Charlotte Amalie. People who saw the woman were terrified. Many of them were making comparisons with the Green Face Man, but in fact felt more threatened by the lady with the strange feet than by Green Face. Probably this fear resulted from the lack of any knowledge about Cowfoot. The truth is, there was no known history about her, and when she was sighted by the children of the small elementary school this was the first known indication of her existence. People had already been familiar with the Green face man decades earlier, and even embraced him as part of Virgin Islands cultural legacy, albeit somewhat reluctantly.

News quickly spread about Cowfoot's journey, and people were lined up at all points along the way, from the Sugar Estate area, along the waterfront,

Lindberg, and Brewers Bay. Some had predicted that perhaps she simply wanted to go to the extreme western end of the island, known to be more idyllic and pastoral. Many conversations centered on the possibility that she simply wanted to graze, that she was hungry and that human food did not satisfy her in any way. As she ran in the streets, residents were laughing at the strange clicking sound emanating from her feet. "Mebela, Mebela. Ah tell yoh she is deh reincarnation of mey precious Mebela," shouted Miss Marilyn, one of the leaders of the mob. Incredibly, the entire chase was taking on the atmosphere of a festival, or a huge party. Virgin Islanders are known to create celebrations for any reason; this was no exception. One of the local bands was contacted and in no time was playing beautiful Quelbe music. Cowfoot, not steep in Virgin Islands culture, stopped momentarily to try to dance, but was confounded by the awkwardness of her feet. "I carn' dance dis calypso o' Quelbe ting," she thought to herself as she continued running at top speed, determined more than ever to escape her pursuers.

The unusual chase, of residents, several local bands, a pack of mangy dogs and a few stray cats would soon come to an end that would confound islanders for years. As Cowfoot dashed for the Black Point Hill close to Brewers Bay through the corner of her eyes she glimpsed a cave. "I mus' geh up de toh dat cave," she thought to herself, not at all aware that islanders stay far from the cave. Her sudden 90 degrees turn really confused everyone; the dogs were howling like wolves, and the cats, decided to abandon the task. Just as Cowfoot started running through the bushes she was met by several cows, grazing nearby. Somewhat perplexed by the commotion and viewing Cowfoot as "weird," they still somehow recognized a kind of kinship with the fleeing woman. The cows began to make loud mooing sounds, which to everyone's surprise seemed to be communicating with Cowfoot, in a way in which the throng could not grasp.

Confident that the cows would not become a part of the pursuing mob, Cowfoot moved slowly, though somewhat cautiously, toward them. They quickly nestled her in the middle of the herd and all began running furiously toward the direction of the cave. It was indeed a rare sight, and in fact, a strange set of events. But above all, it was a special affair, one showcasing the sensitivity and compassion of the animals. Yet no one was able to explain why the entire island seemed to be in hot pursuit of Cowfoot, even though the best guess was that it was all driven by curiosity. Why the obsession? As Virgin Islanders en masse gathered on the nearby Brewers Beach, Cowfoot moved safely with her new, blended family. The children from the elementary school were nearby, cheering and applauding her escape. During the entire episode they simply wanted to touch her, confessed one of the girls. In essence, it was the adults who had turned this into a spectacle, a kind of uncontrolled and uncontrollable freak show.

"I ain' no freak," shouted Cowfoot now from a safe distance halfway up the hill where the cave is located. "Ah say it once, an' Ah want' toh say it again. Will someone respond toh me? Ah is a wonderful person; Ah even dus attend Sunday school an' dus try toh blend in with the crowd wen' it have a large group. Ah dus even sing arl deh chuch song dem—Ah dus sing good, and might even join deh choir in deh future. Why ah you hate meh so much?" No doubt from her shielded position, and protected by her assumed genealogical family, Cowfoot was becoming more and more assertive, adamant, and even arrogant in her vocal declarations. "Furthermore," she continued, "Ah carn' believe ah entire islan' is tryin' toh capture an innocent bein', ah creature ah God."

Many in the crowd were offended that she described herself as a person, and how blasphemous that she would so audaciously connect herself with the deity! They preferred toh see her as "ah ting"- - an inexplicable character in the Virgin Islands cultural history.

"You ain no chile ah God," shouted a Sunday school teacher who never trusted Cowfoot since she tried taking over one of her lessons one Sunday morning.

"Ah dus even read Deh Good Book sometimes befo'ah fall asleep," responded Cowfoot defensively. "Ah garn, ah garn wid mey family, leavin' ah yoh heh wid ah yoh stuiepiness."

"Hurray! Hurray," shouted the children in contrast to the adults, as they looked at Cowfoot and her new friends as they disappeared in the Cave where few Virgin Islanders have ever dared to venture.

"We gon keep yoh alive in our oral history," shouted a woman who was a preserver of West Indian oral tradition and institutional memory.

There was no other response from the Cowfoot lady. But more than fifty years later several children at the same elementary school swore that they had since seen a figure that fit the description of Cowfoot. Their teacher, who considered himself a modern man, accused them of imagining too much, of daydreaming.

"There is no such thing," he told them. In the near distance there was the onomatopoeic mooing sound of cows. "This is so strange," whispered the teacher to himself. "If I did not know better, I would swear that those cows were laughing at me." In unison, the children at the school of a generation later, laughed, knowing the truth that their teacher was afraid to confront.

DEM COAL WOMAN

The coal workers labored for hours each day, oblivious at times of the asphyxiating working conditions, but committed to the betterment of their families and community. These "ordinary" women laborers of extraordinary drive and spirit were helping to construct the infra structure of the Virgin Islands society by sacrificing egos and supplanting them with unbridled optimism.

—"We women must strive and toil unselfishly to help guarantee a new, vibrant Virgin Islands," confided one of the women as she hoisted yet another heavy bag of coal on her head, unassisted.

—"Yes, for future generations," chimed in another worker, skinny as a twig, but working the coal pits with the strength and tenacity of several twice her size.

—"As much as we dislike our situation, we must always remember our descendants; yes, those of subsequent centuries. I believe that in our own way, we are building a firmer Virgin Islands society." This thought was exuberantly expressed by one of the younger workers in whose voice could be heard a deep sense of gratitude for what the elders had done for her and others.

It was a typical conversation among these women whose status was always undermined and denigrated and whose contributions were considered largely insignificant. Yet, they are the precursors of the many contemporary successful and influential Virgin Islanders. Their worth should not be measured merely by economic and material criteria. Instead, it is best measured by the fact that they have created a model icon with its base firmly hinged to a past of sacrifices. The women, their bodies soiled by carbonic dust that so typically characterized their features, were telling another untold Virgin Islands story, another repressed truth. Some of them coughed as they spoke, or sneezed in between sentences, clear evidence that this highly productive economic bonanza was extracting its pound of flesh from them. It was taking its toll on these women at the center of a thriving business, but outside the tentacles of its beneficial reach. They were merely objects of labor, dispensable and disposable instruments of the surging 19th century Virgin Islands international exportation exploits.

The Women Coal Workers of the Danish West Indies later gave way to a cadre of 20th century women workers, who without necessarily verbalizing the fact, knew the distinction between self-centeredness and community.

—"We scrub floors," said Miss Jessie.

—"...and we wash the clothes and cook the food for those with means," interrupted Miss Cammie, usually a very quiet woman who preferred to keep her thoughts to herself.

—"Yes, whatever is necessary; that is what we do," added Miss Rosa, "They call our jobs menial, simple, and unimportant. We go unnoticed. Many think that we have little value," she added in a clearly painful and most personal tone.

These women were ushering in a new century, having proudly accepted the torch bequeathed to them by the tireless coal workers of the previous century. Their labor has produced teachers, clerks, doctors, senators, attorneys, governors, accountants, secretaries and more. They are the unheralded heroines whose stories have been drowned out by the noisy sounds of avarice, greed, and blind ambition. Relegated to the back burners of society, in reality they are and have always been the core of who we were and would become. They are the centerpieces of the Virgin Islands narrative, though often portrayed as mere secondary or supporting characters. Their sacrifices have put in place the groundwork for 21st century women and future generations of women workers.

—"I have to work twelve hours tomorrow," Miss Jessie said to her friends, not at all complaining, "but if the coal workers could do it back then, so can I."

—"So must we," supported Miss Thelma.

The descendants of the Coal Women were speaking truth; they were uttering words of liberation, but not for themselves, but for the many to come. They gathered that day to chat, not by design and certainly with no agenda. In their informal meeting they reflected on their ancestors, the Coal Women. But now these 20th century Virgin Islands women were the new standard bearers.

—"The mission of those Coal Women must never be forgotten," Miss Rosa reminded everyone.

—"That is why I toil so hard," responded Miss Corey. "Hours of washing other people's clothes and of cleaning their toilets. Later, more hours of doing the same in my own house, providing for my young ones."

—"I am a product of the Coal Women. Nothing is too much for me to do, nothing too insignificant. I am committed to establishing something for the young ones. Virgin Islands women have been doing that for years. The labor of these women was rewarded with pittance. Their value has been smothered under the weight of history—a history that too often privileges men, and tend to legitimize only *their* contributions," offered Miss Cammie who was now becoming philosophical and political.

—"Yes, yes," said Miss Esme anxious to join in the very interesting conversation. "We don't question the work of men, but we know that the Coal Women are largely ignored in history."

"Too unimportant," shouted Miss Chrissy.

"Too uneducated, too common, too unsophisticated," added Miss Lizzie.

The fact is, though, that there would be no stable Virgin Islands today without the struggles and challenges that the coal workers endured and the hard work of their successors—the 20th women labor force.

—"The sweepers of others' floors," said Miss Iris.

—"The washers of the clothes of the well-to-do," added Miss Marie.

—"And all by hand," Miss Dorothy reminded everyone.

—"The caretakers of others' children," Miss Jenny reminded. "Cutters of cane, hours in the cane fields. It is a myth to think that this was just a man's job."

—"Caring for the sick," added Miss Jenny again.

—"Caretaker of all," opined Miss Bertha, a commentary that received a unanimous approval seen by the nodding of heads.

—"The backbone of our community," chimed in Miss Maggie.

The descendants of the women of coal were demonstrating that their roles, though minimized by society, were endemic in the structural formulation of the present Virgin Islands community. The Coal Women had convened and had spoken. Now more contemporary Virgin Islands women have honored these forbearers by themselves becoming forbearers of others, of 21st century women and beyond.

—"Virgin Islands women," echoed a voice that no one could identify, "are and have always been the cornerstone of these islands."

—"The centerpiece," another forceful voice insisted.

—"Yes, the cornerstone and the centerpiece," yet another voice bellowed.

They were unrecognizable voices, but they rang out not only with authority but with assurance and experience. No one could say for sure, but someone surmised that one of the voices could be that of the venerable Queen Coziah. There was a clear impression that each woman in the group secretly knew that truth. They smiled, then immediately, as if on cue, continued their daily task of rebuilding and restructuring the Virgin Islands.

BUTTY: THE TALE OF A VIRGIN ISLANDS GRIOT

Almost everyone to some degree viewed him with suspicious eyes. Maybe it was his often intense, peculiar look, a kind of philosophical posture that hailed him as scholar, thinker, and sage. Or perhaps it was his attire of no shoes, several pairs of pants, various shirts, and a rope as his belt. Walking St. Thomas' streets with no fixed destination Butty muttered to himself, in a subtle language known to himself alone, and was a topic of conversation for those trying to decode the secrecy of his muffled sounds. Buried beneath his apparent eccentricity, however, was his brilliance, and the unique skills of an expert teller of tales, a genius, no doubt: "Once upon a time in the noble and glorious Ashanti Empire," he would say, "There was a king who often ruled with a stern hand."

The storyteller's opening lines were always done with an impeccable sense of timing, immediately capturing the undivided attention of his anxious listeners, who would invariably gather around as he recounted African or West Indian stories. Ironically, though, the storyteller himself had no known history; his own individual story was unknown to his audience who sat with unbridled enthusiasm and interest. His personal story was perhaps submerged under the stories of the broader community:

"Wey yoh from, Mr. Butty?" asked one girl entranced by the voice of this brilliant man of mystery.

"Well," responded the elaborator of history and myth. "I am from everywhere, and I am here to speak the language of culture and tradition and to translate and interpret our realities."

"Bu' who sen' yoh, Butty?" questioned one of the listeners.

"I cannot speak to what I don't know," answered the wise man.

"Ok, ok, but den tell us one ah yoh stories dem," requested one of the other girls, who like everyone else was always transfixed as Butty spoke of fading and emerging empires, pride, and human frailties. Butty never refused a request to narrate a story. He spoke about the Virgin Islands, its traditions, culture, societal and political challenges and conflicts. Butty's gift of oral elaboration follows a long, rich tradition linked to West African cultures, to the Ashantis, to Yoruba, to Lucumí.* He was the unofficial laureate of the oral narrative, a true griot.

"These stories are a reflection of ourselves," Butty opined one day, as he mesmerized yet another group of young island children with his narratives of dripping suspense. "They help us to define who we are. Each time that I narrate them, they help us to unravel Virgin Islands cultural riddles and enable us to begin to relocate signs." He spoke with a cadence and a grasp of language that in and of itself was captivating.

No other storyteller in the land could match Butty's inimitable style, his wit, his voice- - so naturally suited for oral elaboration. His wealth of knowledge was humbling.

"My mission is to convey a sense of connection. There is something within the structure of the art of telling that speaks to a greater plan, a bigger goal- - that of preserving culture." Clearly, he was not merely one who recited verses, but one who felt them, and was also conscious of his own role in their conservation and preservation.

"But, Mr. Butty," interrupted a child who had walked almost a mile to listen to this man of mystery, "who teach you dis art? Who make you ah storytella'?"

"No one did," answered the modest man very self-assuredly with his impeccable style of delivery.

"As a storyteller I respond to a tacit calling. What people refer to as my eccentric nature is a part of my style; in essence, art disguised as eccentricity."

Butty expressed this position in the same mild, but convincing manner in which he elaborated his West Indian and African folk tales. He was a man of slight built whose mystical appearance could be attributed in part to the dress code to which he rigidly adhered. But, suffice it to say, no one compelled the children of Buckhole, Savan, Silva' Dolla', Bayside, and other areas to listen to this man. He was like a magnet, with children drawn to him wherever he was spotted in the streets on the island. Moreover, no other storyteller on the island could enthrall youngsters the way that the Master did.

Through his words the West Indies became alive, not at all decontextualized from its history, and entangled in the constant processing and reprocessing of myths, fairytales, and legends. This commander of the word, and preserver of customs and traditions protagonized his characters, breathing into them a potent vibrancy. Each time he left, children had no doubt that this unique individual would return yet another day to combine didacticism with entertainment. They always anxiously waited for that day, to see the master once again take his place before them, whether sitting on a box, or standing and recounting tales known or unknown to them. There was always one constant: the griot's knowledge, enthusiasm, and artistic genius.

"Butty, wey yoh goin' now?" asked an excited little boy,

"I must now leave. I now leave my legacy for you and others. You must now take the mantle, must now tell our tales; reveal who we are..."

"Mr Butty. Mr. Butty," it came from a boy seated in the back row of children sitting in one of the Big Yards. "You is deh best, ah Masta' ah stories."

"Oh no," challenged one of the boys who hardly ever spoke. "Yoh is deh Masta' ah deh Mastas dem." All the young listeners shook their heads in tacit agreement; it was as if they could sense the Ashanti and Akan spirits in the air.

*In Cuba the word Lucumí means Yoruba

DEATH YIELDS LIFE

No one saw it coming, except, of course, the enslaved seeking liberation owed to them by humanity itself. It was a tacit acknowledgement among the rebellious West African spirits, the antagonists of the perpetuators of torture and mayhem throughout the small Danish West Indies island. Only the restless on this tiny island nation knew for certain that the status quo would be rattled by a singular courageous act of immeasurable historic proportions.

—-"I will jump over this cliff," said one of the freedom fighters called Kobla, "I will jump, even though this will guarantee my death."

—"So will I," supported a young teen. "I too know that this will deprive me of any future. But what future do I have anyway under a system that dehumanizes me for profit?"

—"I will join you," shouted an older woman probably in her sixties who had endured the system for too many years. "I hope that I can be an encouragement for all those who can no longer endure this. Those who feel that it is never too late to cast off the yoke."

The masses of people on that day in 1733 were demonstrating their true Akan spirit willed to them by a distant continent whose values were still a guidepost in the Caribbean nation, now called home.

—"Return to the fields at once," demanded a recognizable voice filled with rancor and vitriol. It was a voice known too well by those forced to toil in

St. John's ruthless cane industry, by those whose only reason for existence was to ensure the booming businesses of 18th century Danish West Indies.

But that day in 1733 the normally intimidating commands of the overseers and slavers were falling on deaf, unresponsive ears. The children of Ghana and their associates, and other offspring of the magnificent African continent had made their decision. Their plans would not be derailed that day. This was not a sporadic, spontaneous response of a scared people in panic, but rather a shrewd, defiant and calculated stance. This was a conscious decision to follow the hallowed traditions of rebellion and resistance in these islands. The Akwamu spirit was clearly dominating the air.

—"Back to the field. Back to the sugar mills, or there will be dire and unspeakable consequences for all of you and for generations to come. This is the final order," warned a burly man with a long whip made, it seemed, from St. John's own thicket.

—"I will not speak again. You will feel the unlimited wrath of this whip. You must obey. We know that you will obey!"

As he spoke, in his eyes could be seen a mixture of vengeance and shock: "The audacity of these subjects," he thought. That day the rebels could read his evil mind. But the children of Ghana and other African nations had formed an alliance of unbreakable solidarity.

—"We will not obey. We have a fundamental right to be free, bestowed on us by our African continent. We will not obey. We will not yield," insisted one of the freedom fighters.

—"We will not submit. Out of bondage. We will not yield," had quickly become the rallying cry, and the beautiful sound of resistance and defiance could be heard in the deepest valleys of the magnificent island. People in St. Thomas, St. Croix, Tortola, Virgin Gorda and other Virgin Islands, claimed that they could clearly hear the chorus of resistance, the chants, and the sound of optimism.

—"We prefer death to continued subjugation, to endless suffering and pain," said a woman who seemed to be a natural leader of the resistance.

As promised, the slavers did not utter another word. But their demeanor left no doubt of their intentions. But the woman, who did not even flinch after observing those mean faces, urged her cohorts to stand firm, that death could not be worse that their present circumstances; that in fact there was honor inherently associated with these acts of defiance.

St. Johnians were answering the call.

—"Everyone was born free," continued the astute woman.

Those powerful words were embraced by all those whose bodies bore the evidence of domination and control. And on that day in 1733 under a majestic St. John sun and the perennial Virgin Islands trade winds, disobedience became a badge of pride and a symbol of resistance. St. John, Danish West Indies was setting a standard for others to follow. The rebellious spirits of 1733 left their indelible mark in every corner of the Virgin Islands, and the rest of the West Indies. It would not be long before the message reverberated to other islands, and the rest of the world.

No one outside those subjected knew it was coming on that day. It was that day that the great African continent sent codes and signals that reminded them that they are inherently a free people. No one expected such an act, no one but the restless African men, women, and children, only those in tuned on the same frequency wave. Africa had whispered secrets to them. There was no whip sufficiently powerful to derail the plans of these children of Africa, no chain bracelets adequately strong. No one anticipated this historic moment, except those well aware that only death itself stood in the way of life.

DIVING FOR OLYMPIC GOLD

Leaning over the side of the naval ship the American sailor had barely tossed the shiny 1956 quarter when Edwin, feet wailing in the air, shouted, "Ah geh it." Fist clinched and only panting slightly from his effort he signaled to his friends that he had secured the coin, an even subtler signal that he was the best, and most aggressive of the divers. The soldier had just done what passengers on military vessels or cruise ships had done for many years— tossed money in the sea and watched in glee as the young boys from the Pearson Gardens Housing Project tried to retrieve it. It was a ritual, a spectacle; in many ways an innocent show, in which the boys themselves anxiously looked forward to being participants. The boys had been through the routine on numerous previous occasions; at times as they waited below a huge tourist liner, or below some international schooner, filled with passengers who did not speak their language, nor understood it. There was always, however, a common thread- - the desire of the customers of the hotels on the sea to witness the performance taking place on the stage of crystal blue Virgin Islands waters. Besides the West Indian Company area this scenario played itself out just outside the Sub Base area where boys from other sections of the islands gathered to prove their athletic prowess and diving skills.

Passengers coming to the United States Virgin Islands always seemed aware of the special skills of the young island boys who used their swimming abilities to fetch the money thrown into the pristine Virgin Islands seas. "Divin' fo' money," as the boys generally referred to the art, was in many ways a problematic kind of arrangement where visitors delighted in a sort of spectator sport which no one labeled as such.

Yet, the notion of young local children vying and jockeying for ocean space—a scenario cast in the context of socio-economic pressures– was somewhat unsettling. That day that Edwin, shiny quarter in hand, declared victory was likewise one of tension between him and one of the other boys, a contender for the prize.

–"Yoh cheat'," shouted Ronny. Yoh dive unda' wata befo' deh sailor tro' he coin. Ah wus countin' on dat quarta toh see deh movie serial, *Dorango Kid*. Now Ah ain geh enough money."

–"Yoh gotta move quicka, partna'," countered Edwin, the fastest swimmer and best diver among the boys from the 'Housin' who had just returned from below the surface, this time with sand in his hand.

"Ah make bottom. Ah make bottom," he shouted to his friends in a coded language, indecipherable by the spectators perching above. The heroic feat was not lost on the latter, however, as they applauded in glee when the boy "with the *iron lungs*" showed off the lovely white sand. They had seen what they were waiting to see for several hours, the incredible diving skills of the "*natives*."

"Tro' mo' money. Tro' mo' money, Mista'," shouted Edwin as he and the other boys pushed each other to lay claim to the dime tossed by another soldier. While the young boys performed, there was never any real communication with those looking with naked eyes, or through binoculars. The spectators simply laughed or smiled, showing their approval of the protagonists of the sea. Lost on both spectators and participants was the symbolism of the spectacle, or even its ideological undertones. For the sailors, it seemed, this was nothing more than a way to pass the time; for the tourists it was a prime opportunity to capture with a camera the skills "of the *natives*" performing their West Indian version of *Broadway on The High Seas*. For the little *Housin'* boys it was just an opportunity to show their talents, and to earn a few coins while doing so. The merging of these worlds of opposites on the high seas was never a topic of conversation, nor concern for the performers and their audience. Ideology took second place to recreation and economic urgency.

"I hope dese people toss some mo' money," Darwin said to Clifford as they both complained of sunburn and some weariness. The discussions taking place in the vast ocean blue were characteristic of the inner circle of the friends from Pearson Gardens who were forced to be competitors for the prize; it was a tacit competition contextualized by the poverty seething in the underbelly of the island. It was also a conversation out of the reach of the sailors and tourists who were oblivious to the inner struggles of the youngsters and their families, and was simply content with the physical activities unfolding before their eyes.

It was a typical Virgin Islands day, blue skies, invitingly soothing trade winds, and gentle waves which moved the boys to and fro, as they stayed afloat for hours at a time, waiting patiently for the visitors to continue the sport with no official name. From their positions in the ocean the boys were not at all averse to having different types of conversations- -about sports, school, girlfriends, games, and life in general. They would comment on the beautiful rolling mountain chains seen in the distance and the vast harbor which so much defined the character and identity of their island home. In that expansive ocean they spoke of their limited dreams- -of travel, of working later in life to aid their mothers, to improve their island's socio-economic conditions. They recounted dreams frustrated and stifled by the startling realities of mid-century Virgin Islands. But none of them paid particular attention to the symbolism of the tossing of the coins in the deep ocean blue.

"High tide is comin' soon," warned Lionel one of the better swimmers. "We betta' " head back toh shore." The boys knew the waters well and were not worried about anything, not even about sharks or the barracuda infested waters. In point of fact they were so good, that they were able to judge when the tide was going to change, when there would be sea predators nearby, and when to head back to shore. The suggestion to return to shore, however, was not welcomed by Edwin and the other boys.

"Tro' more quarters," shouted Frako, to an audience that could not decipher what he was saying.

It was one of the ironies of this encounter between the two worlds- -two worlds that met, and yet were kept apart by the large ocean liners themselves that symbolically drew a line of demarcation between them. For Edwin, at least, it had been a very productive day. He had outwitted his friends in every way. He proved the best swimmer and diver, and the quickest boy in the sea. The other boys, though disappointed, knew that there would be other days when Edwin would not necessarily be the best, or even better yet, days when his mother would forbid him from going "toh deh bay." They anxiously awaited those days when they would be able to be victorious, catching coins before they hit the waters, retrieving them before they touch the ocean floor, or performing the ultimate feat- - recovering them from the floor of the ocean— a feat only an elite few could perform. But today's show belonged to Edwin. As they headed back to shore, chatting about their eventful day, he was bragging about his accomplishments, an attitude that caused much negative reaction from the throng of ten boys that had taken the trip out to the naval ship.

"Yoh wus jus' lucky," retorted Binko. "We gon see wa' happen tomarrow." Once on land the boys heard the sound of the ship, signaling its readiness to leave the port. From the distance the passengers could not be seen, but the boys were making plans to use their coins to go to the movies to see their favorite show. The 1956 shiny quarter would go a long way in ensuring that all enjoyed the Dorango Kid in techno color at the landmark Center Theater in downtown Charlotte Amalia. Had the soldier known this, he would have proudly concluded that his mission was indeed a productive one because he was contributing to the economic stability of the United States Virgin Islands.

TRUE CRUCIAN ROYALTY

The little girl had just returned to her house after hours of working in the cane field; she looked rather pensive. When her mother asked what was wrong, she informed her that she had been thinking about a recurrent dream that she had been having, and that the dream continued to dominate her thoughts.

"Wa yoh wus dreamin' 'bout, guirl?" her mother asked, with no real sense of urgency or concern.

"Well, mammy," she responded "I had dis dream dat Ah wus some kin' ah queen. Ah was workin' wid oddas toh change St. Croix fo' mey people dem."

Mary's mother smiled at her daughter's comments, and their improbability, but nonetheless assured her that such dreams are normal and that she should not be too obsessed with what she dreamt. In fact, continued her mother, "yoh should nat harass yoh self. Rememba' yoh is jus' ah lil' guirl. Play wid yoh lil' friends dem an' enjoy yohself."

But all day Mary was thinking about what had occurred, and wanted to share it with her friends but was reluctant to do so for fear that they might consider her somewhat strange, maybe even a member of the occult. To her surprise, the dreams continued non-stop for well over a month. In fact, they were becoming even more detailed, and Mary herself, just a twelve-year old girl, was beginning to wonder if maybe she had been a victim of some sort of devious supernatural spell. Because her mother had confided in some of the neighbors the recurring dream that her daughter had recounted, many others in the Federiksted community and the surrounding areas were starting to wonder if the little girl had been somehow enchanted. Was it possible that some kind of spell was cast on her as punishment for something evil that another family member had done?

Mary's visions became even less credible when she later informed her mother that she had visualized herself imprisoned in Bassin, today called Christiansted:

"Ah see meyself in Bassin jail, togedda wid three odda' woman, dey wus Queens too."

Mary's mother who at first interpreted her daughter's dream experiences as part of the logical youthful rite of passage, a sign of innocence, was becoming increasingly alarmed because as she put it, "mey daughter is startin' toh soun' ah lil' funny. Ah really gat toh take ha' toh see somebardy, toh put ah stop toh dis." When Miss Delia came to the house to question the girl and to investigate her mysterious dreams, she was struck by how "normal" Mary appeared to be.

"Bu' tell meh sometin', wa' yoh ask' meh toh come heh fa?" she asked Mary's mother. "After speakin' toh dis chile, Ah 'ain see ah ting wrang wid ha'. Leave ha' be, leh' she use her imagination; she is jus' ah lil' intelligent chile with ah big big imagination."

In fact, Miss Delia's analysis was confirmed by Miss Amy, well known for her interest and skill in the occult. She was invited to the house to confirm or reject Miss Delia's conclusion. Her words were even more poignant:

"Listen lady, stap' wasin' people time wid foolishness. This chile ah yours look like she geh some idea ah wa' she plan toh do in life. Doan stap ha' from dreamin'. Ah feel like dis guirl might someday be ah queen fo' true."

Maybe the two obeah specialists would not have been so positive if Mary had divulged the entire dream, especially the part where she dreamt of an inferno, a vast fire that in her own words, "wus bunnin' down St.

Croix." Even to the young girl, this seemed rather extreme, bizarre, too much out of the ordinary. So she kept this as her little personal secret, revealed only many years later. After listening to the two obeah specialists, Mary's mother started to encourage her even more, telling her that dreams sometimes become reality and that she needed not worry if the dream was a recurring one.

"Mary, Ah jus' feel in my heart dat yoh gon do good. Ah feel it. Ah might not be aroun' bu' Ah know dat my lil' guirl dreams gon come true one day. Ah jus' know." It seems like that was the main assurance that Mary was seeking. As she grew into a young woman she toiled ceaselessly, along with many others, to eke out a meager living in her homeland.

The problem was that she was forbidden to be educated, a victim of the ideology of race and gender. But Mary did not let this detour her; she continued to work arduously in the fields, well aware of the fact that she had the ultimate responsibility for herself. Above all, the dreams that she imagined years earlier around 1860 when she was a little girl still remained implanted in her mind. She could never imagine, however, how in fact she as a simple woman, product of West Africa and also a descendant of Weedwomen, could assist in the alteration of history's course. She had heard about the so-called Freedom Proclamation made by the Governor General Peter von Scholten years earlier and the Danish King's so-called Gradual Emancipation Program. But, like many others living during that period, Mary was not at all impressed. She knew in her heart that the proclamation, *"All unfree in the Danish West Indies are from today free,"* was not binding. She was uneducated, but she sincerely felt that the legality of the declaration never really translated into reality.

In essence, people were still in bondage years after being "freed", and the poisonous atmosphere in St. Croix was created by policies emanating from Denmark. By the late nineteen-century Mary was "working" extra hard for the Danish planters, her efforts, like those of so many Crucians and other Virgin Islanders represented a boom for the Danish economy, but of course, Mary and her cohorts did not reap the benefits of the thriving economy. There is no question that this was forced labor, and Mary was very aware of this fact. She could never quite comprehend why she kept recalling that dream of many years earlier. But Mary was an astute woman, one who clearly had a keen sense of what was happening.

She was a close observer of her surroundings and listened with a sharp ear to what was being said around her, not only by other Crucians, but also by those representing the Danish Crown. In many ways, her ultimate trump card came from the fact that in all likelihood the Crown saw her as ignorant, uneducated, inconsequential, a mere woman, and of little worth beyond her manual labor to the extent that it was profitable for the Crown. Mary always smiled when she encountered those who dismissed her as nothing, or viewed her at best as a mere object. In some ways she knew that such misrepresentations of her and her race would be in fact her strategic advantage, her main vantage point. "Let dem call meh stuiepiddy if dey wan'," she often mused to herself, "One day dey will know betta'." Mary often harbored this thought without the least bit of arrogance and without even recalling her dreams as a little girl. But she had the clear sense that because she was being constantly underestimated, no one would expect that she could be transformed into a catalyst for change on her island.

"Yea," she smiled, "jus' ah black woman, ah simple black woman."

Many years later, Mary in fact did eventually become Queen Mary, thus fulfilling the prophecy suggested by her childhood dreams. She was becoming more and more disenchanted with what was happening on her island. In fact, she confided many times in her friends, some of whom were also Queens that something must change, that in many ways islanders were still slaves many years after the *1848 Proclamation* about which she had heard so much.

"We geh toh stop dis nonsense," she would say. "We geh models of revolt and revolushun." The 1733 Revolt on St. John was already legendary with the defiant Queen Breffu, and Mary would cite the fearlessness and determination of those in the struggle on that island, more than 100 years earlier.

"We carn' forget dem people," she would say. "Dey die fo' we."

Subconsciously, Mary was inching ever closer to merging her dreams with reality, but now was not at all obsessed with the dreams, even though they were now ingrained in the inner most recesses of her mind.

She detested the first of October, called Contract Day, because it was clearly an unjust policy, and worse of all, the fact that she was not free to choose and did not have the right to quit her so-called job was totally abhorrent to her.

"Wat Ah disgrace dat we have toh sign ah stuiepid contract fo' ah whole year," she said, "wokin' unda' horrible conditions, an' worse dan dat, not havin' any rights at all. Ah tink dem ah say dat slavery wus done. Wat ah lie!"

"Ah big lie," echoed another Queen, Bottom Belly. Mary had formed informal alliances with this queen and with two others, Queens Agnes and Mathilda.

Could this be what she was dreaming about in previous years? It always seemed like her dreams had become submerged as she was pushed by the urgency of the moment. She had no time for symbolism and was primarily concerned with the situation on hand- - eking out a living, the unjust system, the forced labor, the inhumane condition, the dehumanization of a people.

The year 1878 marks an important milestone in St. Croix and Virgin Islands history. The Danish militia, determined to quell what they considered a "riot" imposed its artillery might on people seeking basic rights. But the people, the victims of the onslaught and also of the inhumane policies were not deterred. Like their brothers and sisters in St. John they summoned their West African spirits, suffering grave consequences, but exuding the pride emanating from the great African continent. Queen Mary who viewed the attack on her people with disgust smiled one day when she recalled her dreams. She smiled even more when she thought of the comments by her precious mother: "Mary, Ah jus' feel in my heart dat yoh gon do good. Ah feel it. Ah might not be aroun' bu' Ah know dat my lil' guirl dream gon come true one day. Ah jus' know."

Mary felt a sudden sensation of peace, as she thought of how she could help to change the awful conditions, not only for herself, but also for the rest, of the present and future generations of Crucians, St. Thomians, St. Johnians and other West Indian people. She was no ideologue, but simply sought justice. She believed in basic human decency and pride. She was a pragmatist who felt that God had willed us all innate rights. Those violating the rights of her fellow and sister islanders were, as she put it, "violatin' God plans. Ah sick of it."

Queen Mary smiled again, this time recalling her dreams, now having the sense that maybe this was a calling, a greater calling. She was being ushered into history, immortality without intention, without design.

"Ah jus' want toh do deh right ting. Ah jus' want toh help mey sufferin' people," she said one day in a conversation with Agnes, Bottom Belly and Mathilda.

"I ain' wan' toh be no heroine. Ah ain tryin' toh be important. Bu' lemme tell ah yoh sometin' dat Ah neva' tell nobardy ah dream 'bout ah big fire...."

It was really the first time that Mary was making a connection between her dream and her island's future.

"Ah goin' now!" Queen Mary announced her departure in a way that almost seemed impulsive, but she knew that she had to act. The other queens seemed somewhat surprised by the sudden announcement, but were uncompromisingly supportive. They all decided that they would fight against the Danish Militia, in their own way, and, like Mary, were driven by the will to do right— the strongest motivating impulse possible.

"Ah garn! Ah garn!" shouted Mary.

"Bu' Queen Mary wey yoh ah go?" asked a member of the large group that was now gathering.

"Ah ain really geh no time right now," Mary responded. "Ah jus' have toh do wa' is right. Dese Great House dem mus' not stan' any longa'. Ah carn' take no mo' ah dis. Ah wan' tah match. Ah yoh, Ah need some oil. Ah gon bun."

"But, *Queen Mary, Queen Mary, wa' yoh go ah bun?*" asked a young onlooker.

"*Doan' ask meh notin' 'tarl, jus' gimme mey match an' mey oil,*" responded the great leader, strongly supported by the other three strong-willed Crucians and Virgin Islands Queens and others, shouting in chorus: "*Ah yoh jus' give she match an' oil.*"

Queen Mary took a deep breath as she watched the flames running wild; she saw the beauty in the fire meant to destroy, but knew deep down that it had as its intended goal the establishment of real freedom and the restoration of dignity.

She was not at all concerned about losing her island because she knew that she came from a formidable, determined people, who would gain it back. Queen Mary smiled, a broad smile illuminating her face as she recalled that day that she recounted her dreams. Even though she was now languishing in the Bassin jail, she was proud of herself, not because she had become a Queen, not because she had resisted the overwhelming power of the Danish Militia and government; no, she smiled because she sensed that her act of courage and her abiding commitment was going to have an impact on her islands. She could not prove it, but she sensed it. She was right; the course of Virgin Islands history was rerouted forever because this Queen rejected subjugation and domination.

"Yea," recalled Queen Mary one day in an interview from the Bassin jail. "Ah hea' dey plan toh sen' ah we toh da' place, Denmark, sum place fa' from mey home. Bu' meh ain care. Meh do wa' meh ha' toh do. Leh dem deh do wa' dem wan' toh do. If dem doan watch it, Ah will bun dem ova' de too."

With that Mary sucked her teeth, "ah 'ain 'fraid dem atarl."

The four queens laughed out loud that day in Bassin Jailhouse, knowing that no amount of imprisonment could dull their African spirit.

"We defeat dem Danish people," bellowed Mary.

"Yoh right, mey dear, yoh so very right," chimed in the others as if rehearsing a chorus for a song of victory.

"Dat match an' oil had some power," said Mary.

The Queens, dreamers all, laughed, and the prison guards were frustrated by the fact that they could never ever penetrate the deep secrets of glory that the women shared. They felt isolated because of their little knowledge of Virgin Islands Creole and culture and hence their inability to comprehend why the Queens were so joyous while imprisoned. The women felt empowered knowing that their hearts and minds were never in bondage. If the guards knew how "toh suck up deh teet' and cut up dey eye," they would do so out of sheer frustration caused by these relentless and defiant Virgin Islands women.

THE ELUSIVE CREATURE:
TALE OF THE GREEN FACE MAN

(In memory of my father: *Charles Alexander White, Sr.*)

According to the police blotter he jumped from one roof to another; it was perhaps his greatest talent, and in fact it was likewise his badge of honor and his customary mode of escape. Officer Alexander filed his report early one Saturday morning, hours after he claimed that something had run swiftly across one of the red galvanized roofs so typical of the buildings in Charlotte Amalie during the 1950's. As the officer reached out to grab him, the creature catapulted from the roof to a tree limb, barely attached to the main tree's structure. It was a kenip tree, the branch of which was hanging precariously over the Big Yard close to Princess Gade. That the officer did not capture the elusive being who moved as expertly as a monkey escaping his predator surprised no one; but because Officer Alexander almost succeeded, he was encouraged and energized by the prospect of being able to do what no other officer or private citizen had ever done- - capture the Green Face Man. This creature, who roamed St. Thomas' streets, especially a place referred to as *"Roun' de Coas"* and the Savan area, was a slippery being. Part of the problem, of course, was that like the ghastly bat, he chose the nighttime to surface, never staying too long in any one place. There was only one constant - - he had never harmed anyone, according to those who had tracked his path for years; nor did he had the intention of doing so. By all accounts, his principal aim seemed to be the general disruption of the lives of islanders, to create fear.

—"You are the product ah deh devil," Officer Alexander had told the Green Face Man one dark night when he came face to face with the creature. "Yoh connected toh deh netherworld, deh occult. We islanders see Satanism arl ova' yoh forehead. Furthermore, yoh desecratin' our historic landmark, our red roofs wid yoh crazy jumpin' an' swingin'." Green face, by now accustomed to such insults, simply sucked his teeth, an art he claimed that he learned from local residents after moving from village to village in St. Thomas.

St. Thomas had been known for its appealing red roofs, done as a political and strategic initiative to protect against the possibility of mistaken aerial attacks during the Second World War. To islanders, of course, the roofs had quickly lost their militaristic implications, but had remained as fixtures of a larger socio-cultural institution. These red roofs were part of the Virgin Islands architectural and cultural identity, as were the wooden houses with their structural simplicity and charm. The police found it very offensive that this unwelcomed fellow would be so audacious as to march across the roofs, already by this time, elevated to a special status in the island's cultural tapestry.

"No way," said the man with the bright green color, resembling one of the island's green iguanas. "I ain' connected toh anyting. It ain my intent toh do notin' toh nobardy. I, too, is ah islander, ah St. Tomian, o ah Tomian, darn wa' ah you duz call ah yo'self?"

"Turn yoh self in," pleaded the officer. You have been creatin' problems in the Virgin Islands for too many years now." Many people in Tortola, St. Croix, Virgin Gorda, and St. John had issued similar reports, claiming that they had seen the man at various sites on their particular island. For example, according to police records he was sighted various times in Long Look. And no one could be sure why he always chose the Baths in Virgin Gorda, but the general consensus was that he was attracted by its beauty, the very magic and wonderment of this natural monument of nature. St. Johnians in Cinnamon Bay swore that they saw him regularly at nights. Others in St. John swore that they saw him taking a dip in Trunk Bay, in fact more than once.

One of the ironies about the creature was that even though everyone claimed to be afraid of him, everyone was happy to report a face to face confrontation. At the same time, parents were not taking any chances, making sure that they kept their little ones next to their sides, as government officials tried to devise strategies to capture the man.

There was no doubt that Officer Alexander wanted to be the one to capture the Green Face Man. The officer's children always awaited their father's return home, anxious to hear his many tales about his encounter with the mysterious man.

"I almos' ketch him deh las' time," confided the police officer to his children who by now were enthralled by their father's encounters. Men who related the stories were likewise transforming themselves into heroes, at least in the eyes of their children. In the face of all of the negative publicity, the Green Face Man decided to tell his own story. Sitting in the bough of a robust mango tree *Roun' de Coas* where he had once more successfully escaped a throng of police officers, including Alexander, Ryan, Guilliam, and Roberts, he pleaded for understanding:

–"My face should not be the cause fo' panic and fear," he shouted down to the frustrated officers who could do no more than merely shine their dim flashlights in the direction of the branch where the Green Face man was now arrogantly perched.

"Some people spreadin' rumors 'bout meh and exaggeratin' mey predatory skills. Dey call meh some kin' ah ogre, ah monster, ah vicious bein.' My aim is toh co-exist among Homo sapiens, and be ah doer ah good deeds. Ah you even doan try toh understan' meh. But jus' keep spreadin' deh same ole gossip an' lies 'bout me."

"Give yoh self up, fellow," begged Officer Alexander, hoping, like the others, that he would become the person responsible for the arrest of the Green Face Man, the first to lock him up in the Fort, St. Thomas' prison- -a feat that every officer had imagined for years. Even the most decorated officer could not claim such an accomplishment!

"Wa' Ah do wrong? Ah you tell me, no," challenged the man with the strange face. Not only was it accentuated by the unusual bright green color, but it was also twisted, as they say in the Virgin Islands, "like ah mango seed." It was easy to see why children hid under their wooden beds, or even beneath the old wooden houses when the name 'Green Face Man' was evoked.

Green Face continued as he reflected on his painful experience on St. Thomas: "Dey claim in deh calypso songs that *'Deh Green Face Man is all about...'*"

"Deh Calypsos that mentioned mey name do so in ah negative way. Dem prejudicial songs disparage me. Furthermore, the way the children talk 'bout meh on deh playgrounds an' in deh schools is totally disrespectful. Wus' yet, ah you even doan know meh. It is ah slanderous affair, embarrassin' and humiliatin' for meh and mey family. I wish Ah had deh rights to sue ah you. Ah woudda sue for libel because how ah you dus treat meh is disgraceful."

"I didn' know that you…" began Officer Roberts.

—"Yoh see wa' ah mean; yoh jumpin' toh conclusions again," interjected the man with the twisted face, "Ah doan want toh discuss mey personal life, however. Deh stereotypes an' deh prejudice have defined meh durin' deh past years. Ah want ah you toh see meh like ah normal citizen ah dese islands equal toh everyone else, an' not some kin'ah pariah."

The police officers laughed in unison, as they considered the Green Face Man's plea an absurdity. In their minds, the thought of Green Face as a family man was too strange to contemplate seriously. And Green Face as a citizen? What a mockery of the concept of citizenry. Ignoring the officer's attitude the strange man continued his story:

—"How come ah you dus pursue meh on ah daily basis? Capture deh snakes, mongoose and 'guana dem. Dem de is deh real problems, destroyin' livestock and deh farms on all the islands, especially on St. Thomas North Side. The Home Journal in its last editorial concluded dat I ain no danja' toh society. In fact, I have that editorial with me; Ah aways carry proof of mey innocence. According to the editor of that newspaper:

> *We reject the notion that the Green Face Man is a detriment to our community. It is undisputed that his face is somewhat terrifying, maybe ugly is the appropriate word, but this should not give anyone the license to treat him unfairly. Most of all, he is one of us.*

The officers snickered when they heard the words "maybe ugly." It did not seem like Green Face even acknowledged that particular comment by the newspaper's editor. But they were even more struck by his audacity to identity with them. "One of us?" they mocked. Looking at Green Face they could not understand his obsession to feel like one of them, an authentic Virgin Islander. They could only feel repulsed by the bright green color which for some reason seemed only to get brighter the more he asserted himself. It was clear that they did not need their flashlights to see him, but were only using them to irritate and unsettle him more. In this way, perhaps chase him from St. Thomas, and in fact the entire Virgin Islands forever.

—"Surrenda', Mr. Green Face," hollered Patrolman Alexander feigning respect. "There is no place fo' you on dese islans. Return to deh place dat yoh come from. Wey eva' dat is. Be gone, Green Face, please be gone!"

—"Ah fin' it real strange," countered Green Face, "Dat deh obeah man and woman cou' roam dis place, havin' deh way, an' ah you doan do notin' toh stap dem. Wen is deh las' time dat ah you pursue' one ah dem true members ah deh Society ah deh Occult? An'- plus, wha it matta weh Ah come from?

—"Geh outta heh," reiterated Gilliam, supported by his fellow officers. "Dis ain geh ah ting toh do wid deh obeah cult. We concern' 'bout yoh runnin' up and down our mango and kenip tree dem. Ah hea' dat yoh been even tryin' toh climb the flamboyant and hibiscus trees; Ah tell yoh partna' dat would be ah real scandal, ah defacement ah our culture, dat would be heresy because dese trees are Virgin Islands treasures. An' worse ah all yoh runnin' 'cross deh people dem roof at night, deh lil' innocent babies carn' sleep. Yoh notin' but ah nuisance, ah good fo' notin…'"

–"Jus' one secon'," interrupted Green Face once again, now very annoyed by the comments. He knew enough about Virgin Islands culture to know that calling someone "a good fo' notin'" was a serious affront to the individual's character. "Wait, wait, some ah wa yoh say is true; Ah duz run on deh roofs only because Ah carn' sleep at nights. But dat is because ah you keep tryin' toh ketch meh fo'… Ah still doan know why… Ah try sneakin' in one of dem Big Yards toh see if ah cou' doze off ah little bit, but one ah dem ole lazy dogs smell meh an' start he stuiepid barkin'. People come out deh houses wid lanterns an' ting tryin' toh determine deh reason fo' arl deh strumoo. So Ah jump' ova deh well in deh yard, and hurdle ova' ah broad gut on deh side, and befo' long Ah was safe in ah ole' flamboyant tree. Dat was unusual fo' me; Ah don' eva' climb dat type ah tree, but in dis case it was ah emergency because people wus comin' afta' meh wid dey machetes. Ah cou' see deh sharp edges glitterin' in deh dark. Imagine, dey sharpen' dem ting jus' fo' me."

–"Yoh seekin' our sympathy, Green Face, but we cou' assure you dat yoh will neva' find it heh," one of the officers promised. "Wa you jus' say? Yoh went up one ah our precious flamboyant trees? Green Face, tis jail yoh goin'!"

With the constant conversation taking place, Green Face was unaware that one of the officers had quietly moved to the other side of the tree where he was comfortably perched. The plan, hatched by the police beforehand in a meeting at The Fort, was to distract the creature, then spring a surprise attack on him. The Fort is a structure built during the Danish colonial period in the late seventeenth century and served as the only police precinct on St. Thomas in the early years. It was the ideal place for clandestine planning and for devising strategies.

–"Ah geh yoh," screamed Officer Alexander with premature excitement and jubilation as he stretched out his hands to grab Green Face, who like a world-class broad jumper and hurdler leapt from that tree to another. The officers were stunned. They had heard of his jumping abilities, but this seemed beyond the realm of probability and believability. No officer would admit it, but they were looking at him with uncontrolled admiration.

−"No one will ever ketch him," said Officer Roberts, as the officers stood in amazement.

From their vantage point, they could barely see the creature's silhouette as he laughed scornfully and danced his way across a venerable historic red roof close to Logan Church in historic Savan.

ON THE DOCK OF THE BAY

The boys had gone to swim, once again disregarding their mothers' directives. It was not that they objected to the boys swimming, but that they feared an accident. Yet none of the young boys ever thought of that possibility. They were experiencing the carefree life of children, the false notion of invulnerability. These were young athletic boys who passed the time running, wrestling, roller-skating, playing basketball and swimming, among various other activities. They were the boys in the 1950's and 60's from the Pearson Gardens Housing project in St. Thomas, Virgin Islands. Commonly known as "Housin' boys," they relished the classification that gave them a sense of bonding and unity, an undeniable sense of identity.

—-"Doan go toh de bay," was an admonishment that was regularly uttered by the doting mothers, dedicated and committed to the welfare of their children. – "tain have no lifeguard down de." Incidentally, these were words customarily echoed throughout the Virgin Islands.

The boys always heard what their mothers were saying, even understood their concern. Nonetheless, this knowledge did not deter them from going to the bay, as soon as their mothers had gone to work, or to the market. Swimming was almost an obsession for these young carefree boys. It was always a time of endless fun.

Often as they were swimming they saw schools of fish, or even sharks and barracudas, but no amount of sea creatures could keep them out of the soothing West Indian waters.

—"Les' swim toh dat houseboat," one of the boys suggested, and so they did, in their usual collective styles. "Our mudda dem will neva' know dis."

The boys from the St. Thomas' housing project had a true sense of camaraderie, moving always in groups of three, four, or even more, always defending and protecting each other. Often they would walk to their schools in throngs, talking sports or pontificating on life. Each spoke of life as he understood it, without the sophisticated trimmings of psychology, philosophy, or sociology. They only knew that they wanted to succeed in life. All invariably spoke in high regards of the matriarchs of the various families, and how they planned to assist them once they themselves had become adults. They had dreams that were thwarted by harsh realities, but they dreamt nonetheless, dreams formulated in their own limited worlds, shut off from other nations.

In many ways these children lived in a sheltered world, in large part a world of illusions, made so by lack of access to a larger universe. Discrimination and segregation, Jim Crow Laws in many societies in the United States were barely alluded to in that protected world of juvenile dreams and illusions. The aftermath of Korea, World Wars I & II were mere footnotes. The specter of a corrosive Vietnam was the subject of older more knowledgeable Virgin Islands adults. What governors were being appointed or anointed to lead a people deemed incapable of leading themselves? The children from Pearson Gardens and other Virgin Islands areas hardly ever discussed such matters; yet, as they grew and became more mature, many understood firsthand the lessons of war. Many who swam on the bayside would later walk the jungles of Vietnam, or were stationed aboard a naval ship within close proximity to that country in turmoil. The boys from Housin' were quickly becoming men!

Their journeys were shaped by shared experiences on a playground that knew no timeouts, on a basketball court almost always occupied, except for *those rare occasions* when there were gale winds. If a basketball was not being bounced on the court, then the court was overrun by an endless stream of skilled roller skaters, boys and girls who relished the moments of being with each other. The Roller Derby skaters had nothing over them!

—*"Doan go toh deh bay. Tain geh no watchman ova' de. Ah yoh cou' geh drown."*

So the Housin' boys ignored their mothers' plea and went to the bay anyway, and then invaded the coconut groves, led by an acrobatic boy named "Myie." They moved from grove to grove—Big Grove, Middle Grove, Small Grove, and even the weakest and slowest of the climbers was faster than anyone anywhere else on St. Thomas. When they did not roam the groves, the children wandered over to the West Indian Company dock where they dove for money. Their contact with the "watchmen" always created a point of tension, contention, and humor. After all, the guards' assignment was to keep the "unauthorized" children from entering the area where the dock was located. They clearly also had a mission of keeping them a safe distance from the visiting tourists; keep them hidden, the hidden Virgin Islands treasures. That was their charge clearly given to them by others. On the other hand, though subconsciously, the young boys' job was to insure their own visibility. The dock was their domain, they felt, with no political agenda. They simply understood it to be theirs, and no watchmen could successfully keep them away. They went to the dock to claim what they felt, albeit naively, was rightfully theirs. In their innocent minds, the West Indian dock and Pearson Gardens had no frontier, no boundaries between them. The boys of Pearson Gardens roamed freely, as free as the sparrows and the other birds that soared above.

—*"Stay 'way from deh dock boy, 'specially wen deh touris' dem cum toh town."*

—*"Stay 'way from deh dock an' stay way from deh bayside, boy."*

—*"Ah gon taste yoh hair wen Ah reach home; Ah gon know if yoh went toh deh bay."*

—"I wus on deh court arl day, mammy, playin' basketball."

—*"Who was de wid yoh, son?"*

—"Arl dem Housin' boys, mammy, Diamon' an' Tito an' Paps dem

—"*Nobardy 'ain went toh deh bay?*"

—"No mammy."

—"*Wey yoh geh dat quarta from, boy?*"

—"Ah touris', mammy."

—"*Ah touris' jus' see yoh an' gi' yoh money so? Doan lie, chile, 'cause Papa God 'gon punish yoh.*"

—"Deh touris' tro deh money in deh wata, mammy. Tain meh dat dive fo' it. It was deh bes' swimma' dem...."

—"*But boy, yoh ain' jus' tell meh how yoh ain went deh bay today?*"

—"Ah only walk' by, mammy. Wen Ah look Ah see dem Housin' boys havin' fun. Den, ah see dis money in mey han'."

—"*Ah see salt on yoh forehead, boy. Lemme taste yoh hair. Yes, yoh went deh bay. Bring meh deh belt ova de on deh chair.*"

The boys who were still at the bay could hardly contain themselves when the news of another Scotland Yard mother reached them. Later they admitted that they feared what would happen to them when their own mothers did the salt test. But for now they were basking in the hot Virgin Islands sun, in their own little worlds, looking ahead to how they would outwit the watchmen on the dock who were denying them access to the tourist coin, and how they will try once again to outsmart the mothers and their magical tongues.

DEH BIG YARD: V.I. CULTURAL PULSE

The moon almost always seemed to be full as it remained fixed well above the *Big Yard*, a Virgin Islands fixture, often simply referred to as *Deh Yard*. *Deh Yard* had always had its unique charm, but it was, above all, a communal setting, the umbilical cord of Virgin Islands society with echoes of West Africa. With its customary rectangular feature and its centralized well, it was home to various families, sometimes several households were related to each other, often not. It was a conduit of Virgin Islands lore, news, funeral announcements, wedding notices, and gossip. The pulse of the society could be felt palpitating in the veins of the dwellers. It was also a place of stability where at night "residents" regularly gathered to tell stories– tales of Anansi, stories of jumbies, of obeah men and women, of the Green Face Man. Sometimes members of one Yard traveled to another, not only to visit friends and family, but also to participate in the story telling ventures. There was invariably a tacit competition— who will be the most prolific or talented teller of tales? And, all of this captured and contexualized in a hyperbolic Virgin Islands scenario, under a surreal moonlight, notable for its intense brightness and the way in which it created a mythical atmosphere. No doubt, *Deh Yard* itself harbored its own mythical spirits, its deep secrets – reminiscences of years past, of slave trades and the resettling of families, theoretically freed from the ravages of slavery.

–"I need to move away from this Yard," Elaine complained to her parents one day.

−"That is what you are claiming now, my dear," responded her mother, "I hope that you remember those words as you grow older, for only then will you begin to appreciate your residency here, viewing it in retrospect."

Occasionally people left for the United States of America to seek their fortune well beyond *Deh Yard's* adjacent guts and wooden outhouses. Clearly to some, *Deh Yard* was an asphyxiating structure.

−"This place is confining," complained Elaine. "For me, its circular or rectangular shape is symbolic of a confining power."

−"Quite the contrary, quite the contrary," countered Mr. Ross, a principal preserver of *Deh Yard's* structure and concept. "*Deh Yard* epitomizes security and safety, congeniality and cooperation."

"No one can deny this feeling," continued Elaine. "In fact, it has sustained me ever since I came into this world. Yet, I am beginning to sense that there is an atmosphere of over-protection. Maybe, just maybe, this is what suffocates me and my other young friends. Maybe that is why I sometimes feel like I am limited, unsure of my future."

Clearly, there was emerging in *Deh Yard* the tale of two "cities," a definable generational gap- - each generation idealizing its own situation.

One of the adults, Mr. Eric, took Elaine to task: "Stay here, young lady. Look at that unique moon. See how it reveals itself to us. *Deh Yard* is your main stay, your inspiration. It is your essence, of who you are as West Indian, as Caribbean, as Virgin Islander. It will be the needle of your compass. Do not disrespect this place; do not be ungrateful." All the young children agreed with Mr. Eric with respect to the moon, but they could not accept his pronunciations as they pertained to the intangibles that he was alleging- -the presumed sense of harmony, brotherhood, of community that *Deh Yard* portended.

In the early 1950's when the idea of street lights was a concept grasped by a mere few, the moon was truly a valuable ally, and children above all, appreciated that fact as the constellations gave them more light to jump, to frolic and to play their traditional games of "Jax," "Red Light, Green Light," "Nat It" and other popular island games—the chance to be authentically children. But more and more, the perspective of the older residents with respect to *Deh Yard's* special values was being challenged by a more restless, inquisitive generation. This was a place of constant activities where even missionaries from the United States stopped in to give their Biblical classes and to evangelize the residents. One such missionary was "Sister Esther" who brought her drawings of Zacchaeus and other Biblical protagonists. *Deh Yard's* residents accepted her with open arms as she tried to merge culture with religion in her own inimitable style. As she tried to mold the young ones, she too was shaped by the contours of *Deh Yard.*

Yard dwellers often peeked through holes in the wooden doors and frequently boasted about having seen the sanitation workers who came punctually during the early morning hours, *fo'day marnin*" in the "<u>nite soil truck</u>." This was a reference to those very important and often underappreciated citizens whose tasks it was to transport human wastes. It was a distinctly different era in Virgin Islands history, which was gradually beginning to be transplanted and supplanted by technological advances, concrete wall structures, paved roads, and new interpretations of the world.

—"Yes, there is a mystical union of souls and deep-seated rituals and spirituality connected to *Deh Yard,*" theorized Mr. Ross, the official Yard historian, sociologist, and philosopher.

—"That may very well be so, but I must go beyond *Deh Yard,*" thought Elaine, "beyond the gut and the wooden outhouses shared by so many." As she spoke, the resplendent moonlight began to fade ever so slightly, as it was becoming dark, while simultaneously the mood of the inhabitants started to change. There was a clear sense that *Deh Big Yard* and its residents would be swallowed up by modernization, and spirits diametrically opposed to the traditions, customs, and cultures of the West Indies and the renowned African continent.

THE OBEAH ARTISTS

Mr. Alleck had a questionable reputation, even though according to his own evaluation he was the village's most astute and reliable obeah man. Some customers who frequented his booming business in the lower section of scenic La Vallee on St. Croix claimed complete satisfaction as they allowed themselves to be connected to the gods of the nether world. But unknown to Mr. Alleck was the fact that Miss Amy was rapidly expanding the base of her own obeah business, attracting folk from all parts of the island, including Groove Place, Whim, and Christiansted. Just outside of Miss Amy's yard, written on a piece of wood hanging on her broken down barbed wire fence were the words:

ONLY FO' DEH GOOD AH DEH PEOPLE DEM IN DEH COMMUNITY, NEVA' INTENDED FO' EVIL

It was her motto, passed down to her, she would readily tell you, by her parents, and grandparents, themselves steep in the art of the obeah craft, and, according to Miss Amy, conscientious practitioners of the ancient art. In West Indian cultures obeah is not so easily defined, nor understood though everyone claims to have a sense of what it is, or is not.

One day a stranger came to the fence to request Miss Amy's services. It was a man who looked anxious and desperate. His sweaty face and meandering eyes supported the fact the hc had an urgent request. Since Miss Amy's popularity began to rival that of Mr. Alleck, she had seen her share of desperate islanders seeking her intervention, or as she preferred to refer to her clients: *"sick souls seekin' deh guidance an' care from deh specialist of humanity."* It was a sophisticated way of reinventing herself, to appeal to those who might question the legitimacy of obeah as a transforming art, or who on religious grounds saw this as the intervening hand of the Devil.

—"Miss Amy, Miss Amy," pleaded the visitor who was not thoroughly familiar with the Virgin Islands, nor with island protocol. He was in fact an American not yet acculturated to the islands' social and traditional norms. So it was small wonder that to Miss Amy his introduction seemed rather intrusive and abrupt: "I am in love with someone who ignores me, and I have tried everything: flowers, songs, poetry; nothing works. I love this young woman. Someone told me to come see you. You must help me now. It is important."

"Fus of all," responded Miss Amy, "yoh 'ain have 'marnin' in yoh mout'? 'Cum' talkin' toh meh like yoh know me. Yoh 'ain know me, an' Ah 'ain know yoh, young man. Who yoh be?"

"Good morning, Miss Amy. I seriously need your help."

—"Depend on wa' yoh lookin' fa'," warned the *'Doctor of the occult,* a title that Miss Amy had only recently and arbitrarily, but proudly, added to her coffer of self-indulging titles.

"Read mey motto; I do not perform evil deeds."

—"No, that is not why I am here," responded the American, defending his choice to visit her instead of Mr. Alleck, and hoping that this choice would have a great influence on her decision to work in his behalf. "Mr. Alleck does not impress me, and furthermore he wants too much money to do a simple deed. I understand that obeah can be used to change my fortune. In essence, it can be used to convince Carole that she should be with me. I am not an expert on Virgin Islands beliefs, but that is something that I have learned since relocating here. In fact, I was on the island for less than a month when someone explained all of the rules of the obeah art to me."

—"Listen, Mista', 'tain no way dat yoh cou' learn dis culture in one mont'. Ah been heh ah larng time, since ah barn, an' it still geh' ah lot 'bout dis obeah ting' dat Ah ain quite understan'. Even ah good obeah woman like me duz geh mix up once in a while. So watch wa' yoh say," responded Miss Amy with a didactic tone and proving that she can speak like an American, "our obeah art has been receiving negative reviews lately. It is not, you know, inherently evil, nor should it be used only by the wicked, the tools and instruments of satanic forces. In fact, I see meyself in the tradition of the great prophets, part of the instrumentality of goodness."

—"Fine, fine," said the stranger optimistically and with a dismissive attitude, making it clear that he was not really listening to this staple of Virgin Islands cultural essence. In fact, he had no interest whatsoever in the history nor nomenclature of the obeah craft. "Please, just make sure that Carole respond favorably to me. Do your abra kadabra...." he added, proving that Miss Amy's words were not influencing him in any way.

—"Jus' ah secon', young fellow," interrupted Miss Amy, obviously offended and insulted, "dis 'ain no hocus pocus art wey people duz chant; we doan' believe in no 'abra kadabra's. Let me tell it to you in the American say: *"Incidentally, I don't stick pins in dolls, nor wave a magic wand. You, sir, have a distorted view of this para-science. You see, Mr. Alleck has been fooling our people for years, misleading and misguiding them. People give him large sums of money and leave his name in their Last Will and Testament and things like that, while he promises them fortune and fame. He is, no doubt, a charlatan, you know what that word means? Like a fake, sir, that is what Mr. Alleck....."*

—"Please, Miss Amy, no more talking politics," interrupted the now excited man, once again dismissive and disrespectful, and rather exasperated. "I mean no disrespect, ma'am, but that is too much preaching. Just let your obeah do the talking. I am here for one purpose only. I am madly in love with a local girl whose name is Carole. Please, make her my girlfriend. If you don't do something fast, I will be forced to return to your competitor for some kind of relief."

"Well, if yoh choose toh do so, dat's yoh business," Miss Amy reacted with uncanny calmness and confidence. "But I 'ain gon use mey skill fo' no evil."

—"Fine, fine," shouted the man, obviously impatient and agitated. "Change her features. Make her unattractive so that no one else would…."

—"Carn' do dat, mista'," said Miss Amy candidly.

—"Make her illiterate, unintelligible, 100 pounds heavier. Put sores on her face, anything! No one will like her if you do that, and I believe that this would force her to see the good in me," countered the man, for the first time showing a smile, bitter and cunning, accompanying his annoyance.

—"Carn' do dat one either," shouted Miss Amy, sticking to her principles and faithful to her traditional values, and fundamental obeah norms, and becoming increasingly annoyed.

—"What kind of obeah woman are you if you can't do these basic things that Mr. Alleck has done for years? I have heard from reliable sources that the Virgin Islands community has boasted of his skills for many years, and of his family's success in the business for generations. In fact he is fourth or fifth generation <obeah man>, is that how you say it? Even I, a visitor to these islands know that," said the single- minded man, now mad with Miss Amy and seeking nothing more than verbal revenge.

"Well," responded Miss Amy, with a facial expression that confirmed her annoyance, "I is ah very good obeah woman. But, Ah is ah even betta' mudda. Ah done figure yoh out, and yoh evil ways. Yoh let dat Mr. Alleck an' he many years ah evilness an' wickedness influence' yoh too much. As ah obeah woman, Ah already know how yoh been treatin' woman during the past year or so, since you come down heh to St. Croix. So while you wus tryin' toh get Mr. Alleck toh wok he obeah in yoh favor, Ah wus busy doin' mey own operation, conjurin' good spirits, because dat nice guirl Carole that yoh want' toh deceive and control is mey daughter, and my obeah done wok' on her toh stay away from yoh evil self! Return toh

Mr. Alleck, maybe he can give you sometin' toh rid the headache from dis shockin' news."

—When the word got around the various communities, Miss Amy had her reputation intact, while Mr. Alleck was subjected to ridicule for failing to adhere to the strict operating guidelines of the obeah tradition. His business folded as islanders sought Miss Amy for her wisdom and insight, and they laughed at Mr. Alleck for allowing himself to be manipulated by a person that had no understanding, appreciation, nor respect for West Indian tradition. Last seen, Mr. Alleck was sneaking over Miss Amy's fence, now too embarrassed to let anyone know that he needed the help and intercession of the real *"Doctor of the occult."* Even though there was no proof to confirm it, it was stated that the American man was also trying to jump the fence, having learned his own valuable lesson.

DEH BUCKET BOY

No one was complaining that day about the heat, but it was clear that almost everyone in the Yard could feel the penetrating sun. The children, for the most part, however, seemed oblivious to the rays of the sun, and somehow managed to incorporate that minimal discomfort into their play agenda:

—"Ah yoh need to geh outta da heat," shouted an older resident of the yard. "Arl dat sun ain good fo' yoh."

—"Bu' Mr. Aston, we wan' toh play our game dem, an' tain no fun playin' dem inside," responded Sandra, a little girl wise well beyond her age.

Such verbal exchanges in the Big Yard were endemic of the atmosphere in a space where everyone related as if part of an extended family.

That particular day, the children wanted to play a game, but did not want the adults to become aware of the game because it was imbued with some danger. Miss Esmeralda, one of the grown-ups in the Big Yard, suspected that the children were planning something special, and quipped:

"Ah hope ah yoh doan do anyting crazy heh today."

—"Miss Esmeralda, you doan have to stay here wid us. We gon be ok," said Josiah, the obvious leader of the group.

Once Miss Esmeralda left, someone handed Josiah an old rusty bucket, one that had been used for many years by various members of the yard to fetch water. The bucket, with its customary rope, could always be seen next to the well, the source of water for the residents of the Big Yard. This was officially the *Yard Bucket*. As usual, stray animals also lay claim to a portion of the Yard's terrain, and no one ever thought of curtailing this relationship. Maybe it was just the case that in the Yard, all was respected, or simply that this was the case of natural coexistence. But the idle dogs and bored cats seemed to be curious about the game that to this point seemed to involve an old, outdated dilapidated bucket.

Something different was about to happen, and almost all the children knew that it involved the "*Well of deh Big Yard*," except, of course, Calvin.

—"Jump in," Josiah said to Calvin, "wen yoh geh down in deh well, yoh gon feel nice an' cool. Hol' arn good toh deh rope."

The game, as the children conceived it, involved one of the children entering into the bucket. Calvin was chosen not only because he was the smallest among the group but also the most timid, and the most gullible among these close playmates.

—"Ok, ok," responded Calvin reluctantly, at this point more anxious than scared. "Ah yoh gon pull meh back up quick, right?"

—"Yea, yea," Sandra assured him, even as she sounded somewhat dismissive, "Dis gon be a quick trip. Tell us how deh wata in deh well is. So wenever it too warm in deh Yard we cou' go down an' soak our foot."

Convinced that he was being a pioneer of sorts, Calvin stepped into the bucket as several of the children grabbed on to the rope to help to assure his safety. By this time even the idle dogs and bored cats were gathering around, quite curious of the experiment in the middle of the Yard.

—"Calvin, doan forget, hol' arn tight," Josiah reminded him.

And on that hot sunny Virgin Islands day, Calvin entered into the bucket, holding on to the rope, with his anxiousness gradually being transformed into fear. He was now sweating profusely, probably enough sweat to fill the bucket that he was in. The main problem was that he was on a mission that he did not understand. In point of fact, no one ever told him why he was going into the well, or why he was selected. He only heard vague chatter, generic hints.

—"Tight, Calvin, tight," echoed Sandra, "doan loose arf ah tarl, o' else yoh garn!"

Such commentary only served to reinforce Calvin's fears.

As the bucket was being lowered, Calvin could immediately sense that something strange was going to happen, or at least he would experience something that he had never experienced before. He had repeatedly heard that deep down in the local wells, there was a different world. No one knew exactly what type of world, nor how it was different, but it was common knowledge that there must be something unique in that world below. As the rusty bucket was lowered even further Calvin could see a parade of Virgin Island creatures. First he saw several wood slaves, unsavory lizards that were not welcomed near Virgin Islands houses. Next, he was shocked to see centipedes and their cousins, commonly called "gongolos."

But this was not the most revealing sight; that was reserved for the endless number of iguanas that were climbing the walls of the well, not troubling him, but at least, making him uncomfortable. The scariest moment of all, however, was witnessing a mongoose that he swore was chatting with a snake and asking for forgiveness. He had heard stories about these two from senior members of the Yard. How the mongoose's main job was to get rid of the snake; residents regularly spoke of the "imported mongoose", but Calvin always sucked his teeth in utter disbelief, each time with the same reaction: "Dey aways tarkin' stuiepiness."

—"What a strange world," thought Calvin to himself as he explored the underworld, so near and yet so far removed from the Big Yard of the world above. Now he was witnessing a kaleidoscope of island creatures that seemed more comfortable among themselves. There was something about this sight that was inexplicably appealing to the boy in *deh bucket*.

It was just at that point that he felt as if the bucket was being raised upward, and without even thinking shocked everyone above as he shouted:

—"Ah yoh, hol' arn, no 'cause I ain ready to come up yet."

—"But, Calvin, Miss Esmeralda and dem gon come out soon, an' we gon be in trouble. We mus' pull yoh up now," screamed Sandra. "Yoh mus' come back toh deh Yard."

But the bucket boy, kept pullin the rope in the opposite direction. Once the animals witnessed what was happening, they joined in and offered resistance to the children above. It was most ironic to see the shyest boy in the yard taking control, asserting his will.

—"Ah stayin' down heh in dis peaceful place. Ah love dis world," retorted the little bucket boy. "Dis mey new home."

It was just then that several adults hearing the commotion walked toward the well, trying to get a sense of what was happening. As they arrived, they could hear Calvin's voice, but not see him. The children simply told them that he was playing elsewhere, behind one of the little wooden houses, just a popular Virgin Islands game of "*Ketcha*."

Weeks passed, then months, then years, and Calvin refused to return to the Yard. Each day he affirmed his position even more; the Bucket Boy was being transformed into a resident of the underworld of the Well.

He and his new friends constantly pulled the rope in the opposite direction to insure his long residence in the underworld of the *Well of deh Big Yard*. This all changed one day. Several of the creatures below had a talk with Calvin, and convinced him that his was the world above, even though the world in which they live may seem appealing. It was then that Calvin the Bucket Boy started making his way to the top.

It was also then that he realized that he had missed his friends above, and that the world below, was only being imagined, as he awoke from a long nap, brought on by the unforgiving sun. The Bucket Boy gave a sigh of relief, and resumed his games with the Yard children, but smiled each time he thought of his new friends in that world beneath. On the other hand, his playmates in the Yard laughed uncontrollably each time Calvin tried to narrate his experiences. The Bucket Boy was not at all troubled by their dismissive gestures. In fact, one day just after his friends had finished ridiculing him because of his "weird dream," he stood at the well, staring unflinchingly at the still water, and wondering if the Virgin Islands kingdom was still intact. The Bucket Boy never moved from that spot, and conversed with his friends below in a language that made his Yard friends envious. The timid Calvin became the center of attention even from residents of other yards. The fame did not move him. The Bucket Boy was more impressed by his daily dialogues with the parade of Virgin Islands celebrities in the underworld of the Well of the Big Yard.

MESSAGE FROM BEYOND

The Ferry running between Cruz Bay, St. John and Red Hook, St. Thomas had only briefly left the St. John dock when one of the passengers thought that she heard an unusual noise.

−"If Ah ain' mistakin', Ah believe dat it geh ah noise comin' from the bottom of dis ferry," said one passenger to another.

−"Yoh have ah creative mind, Dorothy," laughed her Friend Emma.

But Dorothy insisted that she had indeed heard something unusual, a sound out of the ordinary. The travel between the two islands typically had been uneventful. Those making the trip had come to expect bright skies, a soothing trade winds, gentle waves, and a retrospective view of St. John's unparalleled beauty. As Dorothy looked out the Ferry's window in a vain attempt to determine the source of the noise, she could not help but contemplate St. John's regal posture, its regal landscape and its glorious history. At the moment, however, she seemed more preoccupied with the unwelcome noise.

−"Call deh captain, o' any crew member," she pleaded with her friend. "I tink' dat it geh some kin' ah problem heh."

−"Tis ah new boat," Emma reminded her. "Dis only it secon' trip from St. John. Wa' kin' ah problem it cou' have aready? Relax, Dorothy, Ah gon ...."

But before she could finish the sentence, Emma not only heard the noise, but felt the ferry tilting to its left side.

–"Captain. Captain Simmonds," she shouted frantically. "Sometin' strange happenin' heh." As the crew began to investigate, they were only able to tell that there was something in the waters very close to the ferry.

—"Cut engine. Cut engine," shouted the captain.

By this time, all the passengers were looking over board with great curiosity. It was quite a scene, the majestic, blue waters of St. John showing evidence of the sun's brilliant rays. These are the same waters which generations earlier served as conduit for human cargo, branded with designated addresses and postmarked with the stamp of eternal suffering. But on this day, the passengers seemed oblivious to these historical realities, and even more so to St. John's indispensable role in the march toward freedom — how the island's inhabitants resisted subjugation, the revolt of 1733 where the brave and determined Ghanaians held the islands captive for months. This information, important as it was, seemed momentarily secondary to a more seemingly urgent reality

–"Ah you," shouted Emma, "wat' is dat?" The passengers were shocked to see what appeared to be a human being swimming so close to the ferry that it appeared to be an appendage to it. No doubt, this was the cause of the disturbance. Above all, everyone wanted to know how it could be possible that someone could keep up with a fast moving ferry.

–"Ah always enjoy swimmin' next toh deh boat dem," the stranger surprisingly shouted out to the onlookers, an announcement that only added to the anxiety of the already stressed passengers and crew. Clearly, they were feeling uneasy with the idea of talking to this individual whose identity somehow seemed unmistakably intertwined with the deep blue sea where he appeared so unnaturally situated. Anticipating a reaction from the curious passengers and crew the man in tattered clothing bellowed:

–"Ah been swimmin' dese seas fo' centuries; Ah make dis journey so many times dat Ah don' lose count."

There was something really strange about this encounter; for even though what the man was saying seemed impossible, to the passengers and crew alike it resonated with truth. It was a paradoxical reality that even years later the witnesses to this event were not quite able to explain. Sure, no one wanted to believe that an individual could be such a masterful swimmer. Yet, everyone was responding to the mysterious man without giving much thought to the improbability of the story.

—"I have been an observer fo' years, listenin' toh many conversations, an' in fact been able toh observe many of deh actions of deh travelers."

By this time the passengers were starting to look at each other suspiciously, now somewhat fearful that the inquisitive man knew their inner most secrets- -island conflicts, envy, jealousy, hate, false nationalism, distorted realities, identity crises. This person, swimming these seas for generations, as he himself later categorized it, must certainly have an insight into the psyche of the residents of the islands. However, it seemed, at least at first glance, that the man of the seas had no specific agenda, no real interest, for example, in exploring human misgivings. His only desire, he claimed, was to swim alongside the ferry:

—"I love yoh boat," he assured Captain Simmonds who by this time was both confused and somewhat annoyed that this person was affecting the ferry's rigid schedule.

—"Listen, Mr. ...... By deh way, yoh have ah name?" asked the Captain impatient and concerned about maintaining his perfect record of punctuality. At the same time he gave instructions to his co-captain to restart the engine.

—"Ah lot ah passengers waitin' fo' us in St. Thomas....," he continued, demanding that the uninvited visitor clearly identified himself. As happened the first time, silence!

It was a strange day indeed as no one had a clear sense of who this person was or what he really wanted. Could it be that he was going to bring harm to the ferry and its passengers? Could it be that he was simply a wayward person looking for help? There was no clear explanation. Was he a spy? Everyone was baffled.

—"I have explored dese seas fo' repeatedly," continued the swimmer, well aware that the passengers were becoming increasingly nervous and uneasy. "I escape'."

If the onlookers were confused before, now they were even more so as no one was able to decipher the mode of the conversation. Escaped from where? Was he a prisoner? And if so, a prisoner of what? And where?

—"Yoh is ah strange person," shouted Joyce, somewhat combative and annoyed that this person might cause her to arrive late to her job on St. Thomas. "Look frien', Ah sorry, bu' you need toh return wey yoh escape' from; but leave we alone. Yoh 'ain geh no right toh be swimmin' next toh dis boat."

As if he did not hear a word, the man from somewhere, or from nowhere, said calmly, "I cou' not take it no more...I had toh leave..."

—"Dat fella geh ah serious condition," opined Dorothy by now convinced like everyone else that she was dealing with someone with irreversible psychological problems. "You need some help, meson. Ah need toh call deh Coast Guard, or Customs, or Immigration, or ah psychiatrist, or ah priest, somebardy fo' yoh..."

—"No, yoh doan have toh do dat," responded the man, a reaction that caught everyone's attention.

"Look at mey clothes; Ah ain change' dem in generations. Ah so amaze' dat ah you duz travel dese waters with no regard fo' who lie below, widout even ah occasional thought 'bout we."

—"Da man sicka' dan' I ha' tink," Emma said to her friend, deliberately in a loud enough voice for the man to hear....

—"Dey lie below, dey lie below the surface of dese waters. Dey tell the real stories, of pain, of suffering, of subjugation. Dese waters speakin' toh you tru' me; bu' nobardy ain listenin'. Deh bones, deh bones. Dey lie below. Dere DNA recall ah history dat is all too silent, arl de history stifled by the engines of the sea." The man was espousing information with no regard to the commentary by the onlookers. He seemed more committed to a particular, unspoken mission.

Everyone remained speechless as the man in rags continued his thoughts, in what seemed to be a diatribe:

–"I surface' toh tell deh untol' story. Ah seek deh opportune moments. I can always tell wen' ah ferry travelin', the vibratin' engines duz resonate below; we duz hea' deh laughter of deh passengers dem, feel the constant ripples below, but mos' of all the deafenin' silence of our historical reality. Dey lie below; dey lie below the surface of dese waters. Fossils of men, women, children. Dey lie below, free from bondage."

The confusion, fear, frustration, and annoyance of the man's audience were all gradually changing, as they were becoming emotional. Yes, it is true that most of them had traveled the same seas for many years without giving thought to history, without thinking about the islands' traumatic past. Inter island travel was a ritual in the area. The tendency had always been to romanticize and sanitize the past, to situate the islands within the parameters of mere physical beauty, and in so doing relegate the past to the abyss of historical distortions.

–"Ah tell ah you, deh bones dem down de, de bottom ah de ocean wid big secrets of St. John, of the Virgin Islands glorious and inglorious past- - of revolt, of rebellion, of challenges toh ah tough system of subjection. I swim next toh you toh bring deh word from below, unsettlin' it may be, but yoh must hea' it."

Mr. Simmonds who at first was anxious to arrive to Red Hook on time, during these moments seemed unconcerned with his stellar record of promptness. "Sometin' more important, is happenin' heh," he rationalized. "Tell us mo'....wa' yoh name again?"

Once more, silence!

–"Mey mission ain' toh jus' fill yoh head wid details of our past, of lives lost, though countless, of human flesh converted into meals for predators of the seas. Ah jus' want toh let you know dat below deh evidence of the journeys is dere. As you tink about deh splendor of these lands, deh flowers and the fauna dem, jus' remember dat everyday ah you duz pass ova' numerous sacred grave sites."

–"Yoh clothes, Mister, yoh clothes... Dem is deh same........?" asked Joyce bewildered.

–"Yes, deh same clothes that Ah use toh wea' in deh fields. Ah duz keep dem on fo' evidence. Ah ain had no doubt that one day Ah would be able toh stop one of deh boats and have ah heart toh heart talk with deh passengers. Ah represent dem below." As he once more repeated those words, he retreated from the ferry, just as mysteriously as he had appeared.

As he dove quietly, a master diver as well as he was a master swimmer his torn trousers caught the undivided attention of the enthralled, and now respectful and admiring onlookers.

–Wa' yoh name mista'; who you iz? Who sen' yoh?" The Captain asked in vain once more, as the ripples of the dive seemed to be sending subliminal messages of sacrifice and hope for the Islands' future emanating from the souls of those below.

DEH BAMBOULA WOMAN

How ironic that Queen Coziah did not have enough coal to heat her own coal pot, even though it was her relentless toiling that helped to ensure the production of this substance for the owners of the booming coal business. She sighed as she thought of how she could be able to feed herself and her family, having not enough resources to garner the fuel necessary to prepare her fish. Queen Coziah was a strong woman, a proud West Indian woman, a Bamboula dancer, fighting to exist during a time in the Virgin Islands when laws inscribed her as nothing, and social policies kept her at the very margins of society in the Danish West Indies. But as a fighter and keen observer she was never resigned to her position as coal worker. This industry in St. Thomas during the late 19th century, the so-called Post Emancipation period, was a flourishing one, and many men and women toiled for long unforgiving hours to sustain this business venture. One day Queen Coziah made it clear to some of her friends and coworkers that she would no longer continue to work under the cruel conditions:

- "Who dis helpin'?" she asked a group of her fellow and sister workers one day. "One ting Ah know, dis coal producin' ting 'ain helpin' deh workers, ah tarl."

-"But Queen Coziah," responded one of the workers, emphasizing her status as "Queen," a sign of great respect, "tain much we cou' do. We so po'; so' tell me, wa' kina power po' people have? An anodda' ting,' Queen Coziah, we geh toh rememba wa' happen' wey back. Wen it wuz? Maybe ah lil' ova' ten years ago in St. Croix."

-"Ah know wa yoh tarkin' about," responded the confident Queen, "Ah know dat yoh tarkin' 'bout deh atrocities dat the Danish Militia do. An', we ain even know how many people really dead in dat attack. Sometimes Ah duz ask meyself, how much innocent children garn home toh deh maker? Nobardy ain like toh tark 'bout dat."

-"We shouln' talk 'bout it, Queen Coziah," said one of the workers, "deh whole ting duz make meh too sick. Po' St. Croix."

It was clear to Queen Coziah that the events in St. Croix in 1878 were having a devastating effect on the confidence of her co-workers. How could she change the tone of the conversation, and redirect the thought patterns of these victims of unjust labor laws? In essence, how could she convince her fellow and sister islanders that St. Croix was a model to follow, and not an example of what could go wrong?

One of the very wise women taking part in the conversation then expressed a point of view that Queen Coziah suspected was held by many in the crowd:

- "Ah gon tell deh trut, Ah scared dat sumtin' cou' happen toh us ova heh in St. Thomas too. Yoh tink dat dey love we mo' dan dem ova' in St. Croix? Queen Coziah, dey shoot dem down, deh shoot dem down like dargs."

-"Yes, dey shoot dem down, dey shoot dem down," echoed a throng of people now gathered, some out of curiosity, others because they were also tired of the mistreatment. Queen Coziah knew that she had a lot of supporters. She knew that her co-workers had come from a long line of resistance fighters- - slaves fighting against their predetermined destinies, constantly restless in their state of bondage. She was also aware, however, that they were paralyzed by fear. She did not discredit them in any way. She was not naïve and had no doubt that if she stepped beyond her prescribed societal limits of gender and race that she and many others could suffer the same fate as those in St. Croix, who sacrificed everything to upend a system of brutality and domination.

But Queen Coziah, as any good leader would, took some time to gather herself because over the past weeks she was trying to think of what she could do to improve the conditions under which they were subjected to work. She was becoming more and more convinced that doing nothing was not an option. In fact, she thought to herself that if no one protested the unfair conditions, low wages, unhealthy surroundings, and long hours, those who oversaw the operation would consider their inaction as complicity. Queen Coziah refused to be complicit in her own subjugation, and in that of her people. More and more she was beginning to feel an unshakable sense of moral responsibility. Taking a deep breath she told her audience:

-"Ah yoh listen, but listen toh meh real good. Ah understan' wa' it is ah you sayin', an' tain have nobardy dat feel wus dan me fo wa' happen' in St. Croix some years aback. In fact, Ah sure, some ah mey family wus involve' in dat brave action in St. Croix. God only knows how much ah dem garn. Ah understan'."

Queen Coziah stated her position, but she was really saving the best for last. She knew that many of these workers had children, so she asked herself how she could use this information to her benefit. Then it struck her. She would try to allay their fears by appealing to what she knew best: that the workers were dedicated and commitment to their children. She recalled in her mind numerous conversations in which many of the women spoke of sending their children to America to seek a better future. Many times she did not respond to them because she had heard that the situation in America was not good for people of her color, of her race. But she did not want to thwart the dreams of the dreamers. What was clear to her, however, was the fact that their desire to send their children to the United States was indicative of an abiding love that they had for their offspring. These were women who were willing to sacrifice it all so that their families could prosper within a system that had set explicit and implicit limits of prosperity for people of African descent. She could seize on the fact that these women would do anything to secure a future for their children.

"America is ah good place fo' dem," Queen Coziah would often respond, well-aware that the relentless arm of poverty circumscribed its victims in well-defined geographical spaces. She knew in her heart that a lack of money meant being restricted to living in the Virgin Islands. Most of all she wanted to be honest with her co-workers.

-"America is ah bigga' place fo' sure," she told a group one day. "Bu' deh trut' is that it gon be hard fo' we toh geh dere," she finally lamented, but being careful not to discourage them, she added, "but Ah know some people who sen' deh chiren' toh New Yark."

Queen Coziah knew for certain that she was referring to people of means, some so-called high colored people. She knew that these were the exceptions, but had committed to not creating a sense of hopelessness:

"Maybe we cou' do sometin' toh help ourself, maybe we could do sometin' toh...toh make life betta' fo' ali we children." It was as if she wanted to sneak in that thought, not give the group a chance to reflect too much; it was a good strategy that appealed to their emotions.

-"Look how Queen Mary, Queen Bottom Belly, and dem sacrifice' demself. We arl benefit from dat brave act by dem woman."

"Yoh tarkin' 'bout dat big fire?" asked one of the women who very often seemed detached. "Ah hea' it bun up ah lot ah house an' ting ova' de."

"Yeh, dat fire wuzn' no accident. Dem in St. Croix do it fo' deh children; dey do it fo' we, fo' arl in deh Virgin Islands," responded the Queen quickly taking the opportunity to put things in prospective.

-"Yoh mean we should bun' down St. Thomas?" the woman asked, her voice quivering. "We so much smaller ova' heh we will bun down quicka'. We gon arl disappea'."

-"Dat ain mey plan," retorted Queen Coziah. "We ain have toh do exactly wa' dem do ova' in St. Croix. Bu' we cou' use dat as inspirashun, foh deh chiren, foh arl de chiren dem."

-"Yea, yea" several in the group shouted in support.

At this time it had become clear that the workers were willing to put their lives in Queen Coziah's hands. It was a strong signal of trust and confidence, and this determined Virgin Islander knew then that she had struck the right chord. She did not necessarily want to copy what happened on St Croix, but there was no doubt that both the revolt of 1733 in St. John and the Labor Revolt in 1878 in St. Croix had its resonance on St. Thomas. Leaders are born at many strategic moments in history, and Queen Coziah was responding to this call of historical urgency. As was the case in St. Croix and St. John, the hegemonic power did not take her seriously. After all, what could a poor, uneducated Black woman do to resist a system of exploitation? One can logically surmise that the steamship owners did not "waste" too much time preoccupied with a possible reaction from the "natives." It can easily be imagined what they must have thought:

-"Do they have money?" It was very likely that they laughed at the very suggestion of such a possibility.

-"Do they have organizational skills?" Indeed they considered the questions as merely rhetorical.

Most of all, those in the seat of power knew that all of the military arsenal belonged to them. But these representatives of the most powerful segment of the society were omitting an important fact- - the leadership qualities that Queen Coziah possessed and her resolve and quest for social and economic liberation.

After she sensed that the crowd was with her she reminded them over and over not to dwell too much on what the Danish Militia had done, but what several women and men with greater internal fortitude did to counteract and reduce the acts of brutality and violence.

-"Dey tink dat we ain know notin' about puttin' tings togedda.' Wa' dem duz call it? '*organizashun*' or some big word like dat? Ah geh some news fo' dem. No, *we* geh sum news for dem."

Little did the entrepreneurs realize that these "simple" African people had ingrained skills that were unnamed, but that were deceptively present, skills emanating from their ancestors. Skills that bounded Queen Mary to Queen Coziah, to Queen Breffu and the latter's role in the 1733 Revolution in St. John to various moments of resistance in the Virgin Islands, and the rest of the West Indies. The owners of the steamships, the purveyors and reapers of great wealth were no doubt determined to continue to sit securely in the seat of power and control- - the epicenter of masculinity and male domination, as well as the apex of racialized politics. In their minds, their quest for continued unlimited control over the islanders should not, nor would not be deterred, especially not by an inconsequential West Indian woman. Certainly in their way of thinking, those who worked for them were "lucky" to have a "good" job and thus should not complain about anything. In essence, they felt that the laborers needed to stop their endless display of ingratitude.

Queen Coziah made it clear that she did not share those views. She knew that the owners and controllers of the Coal Industry could only speak from one perspective – from that of the dominant group. She felt in her heart that they could not identify with illnesses associated with the hazardous duties of a coal laborer, and had probably never even entertained the thought of being hungry, even for a few moments. Moreover, she knew that they had constantly scoffed at Coziah's notion that the duties of the workers were not far removed from slave labor.

-"Slave labor? That is nonsense," bellowed one of the steamship owners. "Slavery was outlawed almost 45 years ago. What are those ungrateful people talking about? What more do they want? Moreover, these lazy people are undeserving of changes." His cohorts all busted out in what seemed like a well-choreographed laughing spell.

In spite of what the owners felt, Queen Coziah was determined to challenge their policies. In fact she did so many times and was met with bulwark resistance. But, Queen Coziah's muse was Queen Mary. It was also Queen Breffu.

-"Queen Mary neva' give up," she said out loud to no one in particular. "I ain givin' up neidda. In St. John Breffu show' her leadership many years ago!"

-"Leh we meet down unda' deh market," she told her sister coal workers, "leh we meet in full force, an' wen dey see our numbers, dey gon have toh make changes."

The owners continued to laugh when they heard of the plans.

-"She is nothing but a dancer; I think that the natives call her the Bamboula Woman, or something like that. Whatever that means in their culture."

But Queen Coziah was not laughing. She knew from her last meeting that the crowd was solidly with her. She sensed that they were no longer afraid, and if they were, they were still willing to sacrifice. Just think of what could happen to hundreds of defenseless people at the mercy of the military power of those who had already proven a willingness to massacre groups of people with impunity. But Queen Coziah was not fearful. She felt that it was her duty to ensure that such a consequence did not occur.

She could not erase the tragedy in St. Croix out of her mind, but she refused to be fearful.

-"Ah gon stan' up fo' our rights," she shouted to the group of supporters all geared up to act. "We gon make it clear that the entire labor system is unfair, deh wages dem, deh conditions, everting. We goin' down de by Deh Market, undah deh Bongalo."

The symbolism of this historic site was not lost on Queen Coziah. She knew what was happening there years earlier; the business of the slave trade was not too many years removed. Her gathering in this spot may have been in some ways one attempt to ensure that history would not repeat itself.

The voices of protesters were strong and were epitomized by a sense that they had conquered whatever fear they had experienced. The moment had come to represent themselves as Virgin Islanders, West Indians, women, workers, and human beings.

As some of the steamship owners and their appointed onlookers listened to Queen Coziah, they were beginning to think that maybe, they had underestimated her "organizational skills." Maybe they misread her color and her gender as somehow a sign of inherent weakness and defeatism.

-"She seemed very strong," said one of them, echoing something about which Queen Coziah's cohorts had no doubts. "We need to meet with her. Somebody mentioned that one of those so-called Queens in St. Croix, some Queen Mary and some others, caused a wild mob scene. These people have no morals, no ethics. I heard that they burnt down a lot of the beautiful Great houses and even some of their own work places. That is blasphemous. But we can't let that happen here. We have too much capital at stake. I recently was eavesdropping and overheard one of them making a reference to someone called Queen Breffu; I am not sure how you pronounce it, but they seem like a bunch of undisciplined women. I believe that that woman is some kind of symbol to them. I don't like how this is going."

-"Coziah," one of the bosses signaled to her after the gathering of solidarity, "we need to talk. Perhaps there is something that we can do."

-"Jus' treat us fair, Mista' Bossman; dat's wa ah you cou' do; jus' treat ah we fair."

-"Let us sit and talk, Coziah. We must talk," reiterated the owner of the coal industry. "I believe that maybe we can make some changes."

Queen Coziah knew that she had done the right thing; she knew that this grassroots protest would be powerful. She had proven them abjectly wrong that day undah deh Market, and in so doing joined ranks with her sister queens, who answered the call against exploitation, humiliation, and inhumanity. Maybe, just maybe next payday, her meager increase would allow her to buy some coal, maybe fry some delicious Caron Fish with okra fungi and dumpling; perhaps, but for Queen Coziah this was not at all on her list of priorities.

UNHERALDED...UNSUNG

Their son, without doubt a precocious child, had early inclinations to use his natural oratory skills, perhaps to become a preacher, spreading the gospel, dreams that were easily thwarted in the Danish West Indies. However, this descendant of the Igbo people of Nigeria showed from the beginning signs of determination, resistance, and perseverance. The seeds of a reformer were being sown even before he was aware of the trend.

—"Ah plan toh leave deh Danish West Indies," Wilmot informed his parents, "to seek mey fortune in another land, perhaps in deh United States of America."

Wilmot, a young and knowledgeable Danish West Indian knew early the limitations of his future in the islands whose economy was kept afloat by the slave industry, still years away from being abolished. Wilmot, through the assistance of others in the Danish West Indies began to prepare himself for a career in a world that largely saw his oratory skills, his astuteness, and intelligence as inconsequential, and perhaps simply an aberration. The Danish Crown had designated him as "Free," an oxymoronic and paradoxical categorization. He was fully aware that the notion of "freedom" did not fully apply to him in the market place of human degradation where such a designation was largely arbitrary. Yet, within the system he was classified as a freeman, being born from parents themselves designated as free by the architects of dehumanization.

—"We gon do wa we can toh help, yoh, Wilmot," his mother had assured him one day when the family was discussing ways to assist their talented son.

—"Maybe, yoh cou' study in America," she had opined optimistically, well aware of the attitude toward people who could trace their ancestry to the African continent.

Wilmot, through the assistance of some people in his congregation tried to enter into some prestigious institutions in America, but was refused due to the laws of de jure segregation prevalent in the still nascent nation. But, in spite of the rejections it was clear that this young man of unbounded ambition and uncanny faith was destined to accomplish great things in life, no matter the prescribed limitations set by the Crown and the obstacles thrown in his path by a fledging new America.

—"You would be ah foreigner in deh United States of America," his father had reminded him.

His young son responded with a smile, knowing within himself that there was nothing that could stifle his dreams. Wilmot Edward Blyden, born in St. Thomas in 1832, was typical of so many more, men and women, boys and girls who thrived despite a societal determinism which not only predicted that they would fail, but also which suggested that by virtue of their very existence there was no remedy.

Wilmot, this precursor of Virgin Islands and West Indian ingenuity rejected that imposed classification and set his dreams at heights that even those around him thought were unrealistic.

—"I plan toh go toh the great continent of Africa an' change lives," Wilmot confided in his parents one bright St. Thomas morning. "Ah see dis as ah type of callin', a sign dat my mission in life is toh transform, toh initiate an' promote changes. Mommy an' Daddy, Ah gon miss ah you, but Ah movin' toh Liberia. Think of dat name, it mean freedom….."

—"But," interrupted his concerned mother, initially skeptical about her son's proposed journey, "yoh ain know ah soul in dat place."

"Wa' yoh gon do de?" chimed in his father, worried that his son would not be able to survive in a place so much bigger than the tiny Danish West Indian island where he was born and raised. The more the parents spoke with their son, however, the more they became convinced that his plans were not only reasonable, but were part of a larger, more pre-ordained overarching mission.

"Ah believe he gon change deh world fo' true," Mrs. Blyden whispered to her husband one day after service at the Dutch Reformed Church, overly concerned that the other parishioners might interpret her comments as vain and braggadocios.

—"Le' dem tink wa de wan' ", added Mr. Blyden, "we know da our son gon help toh change deh worl. Dat is jus' mey gut feelin'. Dis boy heh extra special."

When Wilmot Edward Blyden arrived to Liberia it was obvious that this West Indian man was destined to transform the world from the seat of this West African nation, his adopted land. It is in this country that his genius truly began to manifest itself. Wilmot had returned home, a symbolic journey that would yield fruits for this new republic, not too much older than the transformer himself. The benefits could extend well beyond the great African continent, maybe to the entire world.

"Pan Africanism, freedom, independence, African unity, Ah wan' dese toh be my legacy," said the visionary leader one day to himself in his office in Monrovia. "My first mission is toh insure that we affirm our identity as African people, and we maintain our pride."

Gradually the name of this determined Danish West Indian man became known throughout the African continent and internationally where his vision for Africa and the world was contextualized within a broad framework of humanity, in opposition to what he had known in his native Virgin Islands. The world now has the imprint of this bastion of freedom, justice, and equality – building blocks set in place in a small island, whose Black population was not encouraged to dream beyond the many plantations circumscribing their future and their fate.

"Our son is doin' good tings in Africa," the proud father said to his wife after receiving a letter stamped, not from Liberia, but from Sierra Leone.

—"Dat's our boy," responded his mother with utmost pride "Dat is our Wilmot."

They were justified in their assessment as Wilmot pushed the boundaries of ideological constructions, challenging the institutions of slavery still in existence, even long after emancipation proclamations had been read in many emerging nations. This proud son of the Virgin Islands dedicated his life to ensuring that the notion of freedom was not merely an artificial and convenient term, like the one with which he was too familiar in his native DWI. For Wilmot his own freedom could only be seen through the prism of universal freedom. The Virgin Islands were the staging ground for such a transformational vision, designed and executed by a Virgin Islander and West Indian man who refused to be asphyxiated by policies aimed at dehumanizing people who simply sought a life of decency and justice.

Word on the street of the Danish West Indies was the Wilmot had left to seek a fortune and had been doing well in his new home. Islanders received the news with pride, chatting regularly with the Blyden family to find out more about young Wilmot's journey and achievements.

"Ah believe dat our boy is adjustin' well to dat new place," said Mrs. Blyden, bursting with pride; he is also learning various languages.

"We neva' doubt dat Wilmot wou' do good tings in life," echoed his father, with a glimmer in his eye that was evidence of his sincerity.

"Wat ah honor fo' ah you an' our Virgin Islands," shouted someone in the crowd. "Liberia gon benefit from Wilmot."

"An' Wilmot gon benefit from Liberia an' arl ah Africa," said someone else gathered in front of the Blyden's home, close to the Historic Durch Reformed Church.

It was becoming abundantly clear that this product of the West Indies would be making waves throughout Africa and the world. Wilmot had left to seek his fortune, a mere two years after the 1848 Emancipation Proclamation in the Danish West Indies. His daring move was inspirational for his fellow and sister islanders. Such transcendental figures must never be subjugated in history, in the history of the Virgin Islands with heroes and heroines too often buried beneath the rubbles of a constant collective amnesia.

THE RELENTLESS JUMBIE

It did not take them long to realize that taking that short cut was an ill-advised decision when they found themselves on one of the narrowly paved sidewalk in the place islanders simply referred to as the *Buryin' Groun'*. It was Cheryl's suggestion to walk through this resting place where souls quietly reposed. Her sisters, Corrine, Claudette, and Carolyn however, had argued passionately against the suggestion but was overruled by the older sisters who simply wanted to impose their will. It was a dark night and the moon was eagerly trying to perform its regular duties, that of accentuating St. Thomas' natural landscape. It was an effort far short of successful, frustrated by the challenges of the low mean clouds. At best the moon could only play second fiddle, a secondary character to the main protagonists– the gloomy overcast skies, thunder, and lightning. That night, the ocean, its waters normally smiling when contacted by the moon's gentle rays, lay dormant, all alone. It was an unlikely night for island residents to leave their houses, well aware of their island's cultural history and adherence to myths.

–"Ah cou' hardly see any ah you," whispered Daphne to her sister Charlene. "Ah only have ah sense dat ah yoh wid me, at leas' dats wa' Ah hopin'."

–"Doan be silly," responded her sister Carmen, a professed realist. "Arl ah you exaggeratin' deh so-call' mysterious aspects ah deh graveyard. I ain' believe none ah dat graveyard stuiepidness. In fact 'tis ah peaceful and quiet place heh. Wa' cou' happen toh we? Ah carn' understan' why everybardy in the Virgin Islands tink dat walkin' tru ah graveyard at night is such ah big ting. It is jus' like walkin' in ah quiet park."

But what a night it was! The stars were not taking their customary positions in the sky, perhaps for fear of the cacophonic sounds emanating from the loud crackling noise of thunder. Or could it be that they felt themselves unable to match the whimsical itinerary of the thunder accompanying the lighting strikes? In any case, on such a ghastly evening residents chose wisely to stay at home, except these girls, who were warned by their brothers Clayton, Clarence, and Colville. But they ignored them.

—"Yoh in front ah me?" asked Daphine of any one of her sisters. She was so afraid that she was barely concentrating.

—"Doan' know, carn' see you," reacted Charlene. "I should ah listen toh mey odda sista dem, Corrine and Carolyn, and mey brothers, Charles and Celestino who tell meh not toh leave deh house."

—"Not so loud," warned Daphne, her voice now quivering, and with hardly sufficient energy to finish her thought, "I see somethin' strange....."

"Man, stop bein' silly," interrupted Carmen totally frustrated. "Ah you lettin' superstition guide an' control ah you."

—"Say wa' yoh want," continued Daphne "but Ah know wa' ah seein,' an' as fa' as I concern,' right now Ah see three eyes starin' meh."

In West Indian graveyard philosophy this is clear indication of jumbie activity. Every West Indian knows that. The entire Virgin Islands community is well aware of this fact, but no one ever wants to admit it. It is simply a part of the unwritten Virgin Islands traditional norms. On this hazy evening, cultural ideology was colliding with personal posturing. None of the girls was willing to make specific reference to the mysterious West Indian being. The notion is too unsettling, too conflictive.

—"Someone else is wid us," opined Charlene well aware of who that "*someone*" was but terrified at the idea of pronouncing that word.

In the annals of Jumbie ideology and literature the approach to solving this problem is straightforward and direct. According to the latest **Jumbie Encyclopedia**, p. 212:

> *"Toh get rid of ah Jumbie, turn yoh back toh he, spinnin' tree*
> *Times and shoutin' 'jumbie, jumbie.' Den yoh will be set free."*

Cheryl reminded her sisters of the existence of these valuable books on the jumbie, and jumbie etiquette, but the other girls had no interest in cultural philosophy in this moment of panic and crisis. Doris, the eldest and most level headed of the sisters, urged them to relax, that "everyone was bein' too testy." However, before another word was uttered by any of the sisters, without making overt signals to each other, the girls were seen racing out of the grave site. In less than two minutes they were already headed east on St. Thomas' Waterfront, knowing that Jumbie was in hot pursuit. None of the girls dared to look back, however, because it is believed that one should never look back at a jumbie. They ran through the Barracks Yard area, and ironically, were headed close to another gravesite in the Hospital Ground. Well aware of this, the girls shifted gears. St. Thomas' hills offer physical challenges that hardly anyone welcomes; so it was no surprise that the girls were sweating and panting as they thought of the prospect of negotiating Bunker Hill, a steep grade with its unforgiving winding contours. But with Jumbie, steadily gaining the upper hand, no one had time to brood over the huge Virgin Islands mountain chains awaiting them..

–"Ah don' tired," Carmen cried.

–"Me too," responded Cheryl, "but tis deh hill, o' deh Jumbie."

With that, the pace grew even more intense as the girls were beginning to feel that they were losing the competition to Jumbie. They dodged, feinted, and made other jerky moves, but the pesky spirit would not retreat, would not relent.

–"Maybe he gehin' tired too," shouted Charlene to Daphne, hoping that this declaration would in some mysterious way transform itself into a new reality.

–"Jumbies doan geh tired; dey cou' run foreva, widout wata,' widout rest," responded Doris, still remembering everything about jumbie ethics and philosophy, despite her many years living in the United States. The surprise was that she was supported by Carmen, the skeptic who had condemned the others for being too culturally sensitive.

–"Tain you who say bu' how dis jumbie ting is all nonsense?" said Cheryl to her sister, between gasping breaths.

–"I neva say such ah ting; yoh understan' meh wrang. Anyhow, Ah 'ain geh no time fo' idleness. Ah want toh save meyself from da evil spirit. Run fasta' guirls, run fasta," she urged, panting like a wolf just having lost its prey after a long pursuit.

All this conversation and movement created an exasperating situation for the pursued, but not at all for the pursuer whose eyes seemingly continued to grow, whose face seemed bent out of shape, and who was constantly making a strange unrecognizable sound, a cross between laughter and jeering. No one in the Virgin Islands has ever been able to figure out what a jumbie would do if he caught his "victim." But no one wanted to be the subject of experimentation. It had already been 45 minutes or so since the chase started, but it appeared much longer to the girls who by this time were asking if they were chosen randomly. Of course, the answer was simple- - they were chosen for violating cultural norms, tacitly written in the psyche of islanders: **NO ONE ENTERS THE GRAVEYARD AT NIGHT**! This, incidentally, is explicitly stated in the same Jumbie Encyclopedia, cited by Cheryl earlier.

By this time along the route some residents were shouting words of encouragement from their houses. Some were shouting through half-opened windows, others were simply peeking through little cracks in their wooden houses, all guided by fear.

–"Dodge, duck," an elderly gentleman shouted. "Jumbies carn' ben.' Dey inflexible characters."

Other citizens were informing the girls of the closeness of the spirit. "Jus' ah few yards from yoh now," shouted a man named Reovan. "Doan' leh him touch yoh; if ah jumbie touch yoh, partna,' Ah 'fraid dat's it fo' you. Yoh garn!!"

Surprisingly, there were a few residents (some people considered them unsavory characters) who were actually cheering for Jumbie:

"Move Jumbie, move; yoh cou' reach deh smallest one. Doan quit. If yoh stretch out yoh han', yoh cou' get ha," shouted Mr. Alleck, later identified as a prominent practitioner of the obeah craft; he was a wicked man always with a sinister agenda. His friend and sister obeah woman and accomplice, Miss Stella, chimed in:

–"Dem people must ah done sumtin' wrang. Jumbie doan chase people fo' spite. People give dem jumbie ah bad reputation fo' notin'. Dey shoudda stay home like deh odda' sista,' Clarice, an' dey wouln' be in dis mess."

But this evening there will be no slowing down by the desperate young girls who by now with their blazing speed were passing late model, 1950's vehicles, of all types. Motivated by fright and their unsettling notions of what a jumbie portended, the girls had practically circled most of the island, committed to not allowing the spirit to capture them. Still panicking and more confused than before, they were unaware of the fact that they were headed once again toward the same burying site from where they had left, fearing for their lives. They were headed back, subconsciously, toward the site where they started their long run, a run without direction, without a strategy. The violation of cultural norms was having its consequences.

–"We geh toh get rid ah dis ting, guirls, we have toh do it now," said Claudette as they neared the *Buryin' Groun'*, known also by the locals as the *Western Cemetery*. She had unexpectedly now taken the lead after an unexplained sudden burst of speed. By this time Jumbie, that undefined spirit was closing in; they could also feel his breath blowing uncomfortably on their skin. And yes, that laughter was becoming more pronounced, an unmistakable trait of the jumbie.

The spirit was now assuming his inevitable success, and was envisioning his moments of acknowledgment and recognition at the next *Jumbie Summit*, or the next scheduled *Jumbie Association Meeting*. It would be there that he would be able to tell his tale of adventure, and how he had been able to chase several girls that had the audacity to occupy his space in the *Buryin' Groun.*' In fact, anticipating an award, Jumbie was preparing his official words of appreciation in his mind. Ironically enough, however, as Jumbie was visualizing his own fame and fortune, he too was committing a fundamental, fatal error.

As the girls galloped toward the cemetery screaming in anguish, they were also devising their own plan. It was a plan that did not even cross Jumbie's mind, because all along the escape route he was underestimating the girls' connection with their culture, despite their shortcomings. But he himself was about to violate Virgin Islands cultural morays, to ignore the unwritten laws of tradition and customs. As they finally entered through the cemetery gates, on the same narrow sidewalk they tricked Jumbie by slowing down and luring him even closer to them. The spirit, now convinced of his future stardom in the annals of Jumbie literature, reached out to grab one of the girls, Carmen, unaware that they had moved next to a freshly dug hole. Jumbie fell for the basic trick, known by any island child. With a kind of automated reflex, Carmen, the most unlikely conservator of West Indian tradition, uttered the words that sealed Jumbie's fate:

"*Jumbie, Jumbie,*" she recited while spinning three times and turning her back to the spirit just like the encyclopedia had stated.

Suddenly the spirit jumped into his hole, grumbling and mumbling, maybe in part, disappointed that he had missed the unique opportunity to become the most famous Jumbie. The girls meanwhile were set free, and wasted no time in recounting to each other their ordeal, while enjoying the sweet "*tarmon*" in the same cemetery under a century year old tree.

1733 INSURRECTION—
COROMANTEES AN MO'

The entire enslaved population knew that change was in the air. But they were sworn to secrecy by an unwritten code of survival. Danish troops regularly walking the beat in the Danish West Indies could not decipher the code of silence:

—"Walking these *gades** here on St. Thomas I sense the peace and tranquility of the natives in these islands," said one of the guards.

—"Yes," responded the other one, "they are quite a docile people whose psychological make-up guarantees constant, lasting calm."

—"Tamed, docile," laughed the first man.

The soldiers, as was quite characteristic, had dismissed any possibility of insurrection in the DWI, and laughed relentlessly at the thought of tiny St. John having the audacity to challenge the entrenched structure of the institution of slavery.

—"Sometimes I am so bored here," offered one of the veteran soldiers. "The slaves are easy to control. We have our methods of domestication."

—"Do you mean domination?" inquired a recent soldier to the DWI. "The good thing is that they are incapable of devising plans to free themselves."

—"Actually, I mean that savages have to be brought to civilization, very much like the other wild animals. That is why I spoke of domestication."

—"Now I understand," responded the other soldier "the fact is we have access to the lovely beaches and we have free labor. Are they even aware that there are free people in the world?"

— "I don't know," said one of the troops silently listening, "but I will not be the one to tell them," he laughed, a devilish laughter that made it clear that he had no intention of enlightening anyone about anything.

After the conversation the men did their usual routine and went to one of the well-known beaches. Little St. John with its pacific slaves, what can they do? This was the typical line of thinking of the Danish soldiers.

—"Peace, tranquility, calm on my beautiful St. John where the natives are never restless," shouted one of the men while celebrating with a cup of cane rum, a product gleaned from the labor of the enslaved people.

"Access to everything," sang one of the soldiers in a garrison in Cruz bay, emphasizing the word '*everything*.'

The soldiers in the garrison could not imagine that communication among the slave population could be so perfected that it could exclude them, representatives of the hegemonic authority. —"Let dem boas'," whispered one of the enslaved coromantees.

"Leh dem believe wa' eva' dey want." Those subjected to the acrimonious behavior of the Danish crown were having their own conversations. It did not matter to them how the Danish government was interpreting them. Their concern was for their community and how to overcome the subjugation in the midst of overwhelming oppositional military power.

—"We ready," whispered a young Coromantee St. Johnian. —"We ready toh go," responded some men and women hiding in the thicket of some bushes.

—"I wonder what the Africans are up to on St. John?" asked one soldier of another in Christiansted.

—"I know that they are not reading," retorted another with scorn at the idea of a literate African.

The laughter echoed throughout the Danish West Indies.

—"Ah you, we ready," remarked an older St. Johnian, anxious to join in the struggle for freedom. He was always restless, and had been longing for the opportunity to express himself in a more revolutionary manner. St. Thomas and St. Croix were very calm, giving even more encouragement to the Danish garrisons on St. John. It was, even though they did not know it then, the calm before the storm.

—"I love our beaches here," rejoiced a soldier sitting outside of Fort Federick in Federiksted.

—"We ready," a young Ashanti relayed to his group.

—"Beautiful St. Thomas," said a brand new Danish arrival. "I think that I will stay here for a long time, even after my tour of duty is completed."

—"Majestic St. John," sang a veteran soldier, looking over the steep glorious mountain chains.

"What a life! What a life!" shouted one of the soldiers walking the streets in St. Thomas

—"We ready, meson," the leader of the Gold Coast slaves affirmed.

—"Les'go," the echo of these words rang throughout the deep rolling hills in the land where domestication and domination were never accepted by the African populace.

—"What a quiet day!" said one unsuspecting sentry at the garrison.

—"What a calm people!" the superintendent of the garrison bragged. "What a perfect day!"

—"Ah you les go," the leader of the revolt shouted. "Dis is the day."

—"What a peaceful island, this St. John," bragged another soldier.

—"Yes, ah you. This is our day, meson!! We don wait long enough," whispered an Ashanti rebel, quite a distance away from the Danish troops.

"Yea ah yoh, yea," was the resounding chorus in St. John regal hills. "Deh time is heh!

"Sweet, Edenic St. John, my island," insisted one of the soldiers, confident that his role in the perpetuation of the profitable system would not never be upended.

"No more. No more," was the loud, unifying and defiant chorus that was announcing a New Day" in St. John, a New Era in the Danish West Indies." These voices were becoming more and more ominous. St. John would never be the same. Africans-St. Johnians were assuring this on the fateful day in 1733.

**The word *Gade* means street in Danish

DEH BOX FROM NOWEY

It was a girl named Wilma who first claimed that she saw it, as she walked leisurely on St. Thomas Waterfront with her friend, Carol. According to the two girls the object seemed to be moving; yet there was no one touching it. At first, Wilma assumed that it was being tossed about by the wind. But, this was a very calm day on St. Thomas. The local radio station had just announced bright, sunny skies, with an "insignificant breeze," the announcer had said. It was the type of day that islanders had come to expect. The two girls were therefore somewhat puzzled as to why the object would move from one side to another with no external force pushing it.

–"Ain no way dat ah box would be able toh move like dat widout bein' push' or pull', said Wilma to her friend.

— "Unless, of course, someone or someting strange inside," echoed her playmate. The girls were not the only two people who were witnessing this phenomenon, however. In point of fact, by this time many people were beginning to gather on the Waterfront, from where one could witness the breathtaking harbor, the magnet for ships and schooners from all areas of the globe, the gateway centuries ago for the transportation of human cargo. The cliffs hanging proudly proclaimed themselves more majestic than the ocean over which they perched. The gentle waves meandering in the wide-open harbor seemed at best oblivious to the crowd and the noise surrounding the box of mystery. Almost everyone was getting into the act, trying his or her best unscientific methods to guess the origin, nature, and contents of the object.

The whisperings about the box were relentless.

"Ah believe dat it follow' someone from Guadalupe toh St. Thomas," an elderly gentleman said. "I know 'bout dese tings. Deh box heh on ah mission. It must be respected, or else...."

"Or else, wa'?" asked Carol nervously at this point, clearly a little bit afraid of what the mission might be.

The people gathered on the Waterfront included police officers who walked a short distance from the *Fort*, sometimes called *The Red Wall*, once they sensed the commotion. It was rare to see so many people in that area, except if there was a huge fish sale, or if people were trying to catch a ferry to go to the August Monday Festivities on beautiful Tortola. One officer had guessed incorrectly that it was a fistfight, not at all unusual during those days of the late 1950's.

"Haiti, Dominican Republic, the West End of St. Thomas, St. Croix, St. John ....." Without a solid base the onlookers were trying to pinpoint the box's point of origin. It is important to note, though, that no one dared to position himself, or herself, too close to the box. It was then that someone in the crowd began to explain what was really going on. The crowd, including the two young girls, stood incredulously (some were even crying) as a pale woman in a long white dress began to interpret the box's history:

—"It mus' ah follow' somebardy who do ah evil deed," surmised the lady, whose name no one knew. "It ha' toh be someone who devise' ah plan, ah wicked plan." The idea, the woman said confidently was to "bring harm toh ah enemy."

Everyone in the West Indies had heard such stories before. But this woman as she related it seemed so sincere, so earnest, so much aware of the circumstances surrounding the entire mystery. The more she spoke, the more the box moved, edging closer and closer to the edge of the dock. Before she could continue, the box had "jumped" (the word preferred the bystanders) into the water. No one had ever witnessed anything like this before.

"It look' like it swimmin'," shouted one man who seemed more terrified than everyone else. "Ah know that dese tings duz float. But Ah tell you dat box swimmin'."

That day among the local crowd were United States sailors who made regular trips to the islands on huge destroyers that symbolized the militaristic might of the United States. The soldiers, spent much time on the islands but were culturally detached, and by all accounts generally disinterested in the islands' traditions. Several of them made the decision to dive into the water to recover the box, not the least bit concerned about the commotion over the box's mysterious nature, or its para culture- - or perhaps more accurately lacking any sense of connection to the commotion directly related to the islands' customs and beliefs.

—"I am a diver with the United States Navy," said one, in an arrogant tone that was all too familiar to local residents. "I was trained with the UDT." Those initials in mid twentieth century Virgin Islands evoked respect because of the skills of the divers. But before he could jump into the sea the box had already made its way on top of a sailboat, tied up at the dock.

—"This is a trick," shouted the navy man, convinced that his experience as a US naval officer qualified him to understand and interpret any phenomenon any place that his fleet was stationed. But he was soon to find out that what he was witnessing was against the rules of military engagement, against the rules of the sea, against the rules of nature. He quickly learned that the box was not allowing anyone to come too close. Culture became in that moment impenetrable by his skills as a UDT, impenetrable by the power or will of the United States.

—"You see," continued the pale woman in the white dress, "evil is now takin' control. It can only mean that deh box now sense dat deh victim is nearby."

Such commentary provoked great fear in the crowd as everyone began to wonder if he or she was the target of this evil mission. By this time the two girls had made their way through the crowd and were headed toward the Long Bay area, motivated by a deep fear and distrust of the box.

Because they left the Waterfront the girls were not aware of the fact that hundreds of people had already gathered to get a glimpse of the box. All the police officers and firefighters were there. The Home Guards were left alone to solve any crime that might occur in other areas of the island. The Home Guards were not particularly anxious to play the role of island police because they had no weapons. Yet, by all accounts on that day they held their own. There were a few reports of children missing school, and some stealing apples from a store named The Criterion, but beyond that there was nothing major to report. People were shoving, elbowing each other to get a better look at the box. In order to gain a better vantage point some local fishermen had maneuvered donkeys, carrying fresh fish and plantains, to a closer position. The donkeys suddenly began to bray, a sound characteristically different to the normal sounds that we hear from those in the country, close to the Dam and other areas. They were making a long, wailing noise:

"Dey sense deh evilness," continued the woman, clearly a kind of soothsayer, or predictor of the future. "Someone heh is deh target; deh Box done fin' deh victim it was lookin' fa'."

With that the crowd slowly started to disperse. Even the Naval soldiers seemed to be beginning to respect what was happening. At the very least it seemed as though they were somehow becoming more sensitive to this cultural event, or beginning to admit that some cultural norms were beyond the scope and reach of military intervention.

"I think I am ready to return to the ship," said one of the soldiers as he eyed the Box suspiciously through the corner of his left eye. The truth was, he confessed to a friend later, he was afraid to look at the Box with both eyes.

The Box, then suddenly disappeared.

"It went on dat boat," said one of the witnesses, personalizing the object.

—"No, it dive unda' deh wata," countered another, who refused to use the word "sink."

The fact was that no one really saw what happened. The only reality was that the Box was out of sight, just as mysteriously as it had appeared. As the crowd moved away, everyone was doing so backward, trying to keep a close eye on the area where the "ting" (as they were now referring to it) had vanished.

"The Box don' claim' one ah we," announced the woman in the long, wrinkled white dress. As she spoke, someone said that her feet seemed rather unusual, like the feet of a cow. Later the consensus was that the individual making that comment was exaggerating. In fact, when Deh Cowfoot Woman heard the news, she was very offended, claimin' "Ah ain had notin' toh do wid da melee."

"The Box don' claim' one ah we," repeated the spectator in the long white dress, taking a mental census to see who was missing, as the crowd moved away. Since that day, few people talked about the Box, afraid that they might resurrect debates, concerning whether or not the Box had completed its mission. The two girls were laughed at by their playmates in a place called Housin' as they recounted the unbelievable tales of fantasy, about the Box, about its erratic movements. They joined a group of girls and boys playing softball and tried to share with them the mysterious details. No other child in the area where they lived believed a word that they were saying.

–"One day yoh gon arl see," warned Wilma as she threw a strike past one of the doubters.

–"Yea," supported Carol, "it will be a part of Virgin Islands belief system."

That night both girls dreamt that they had opened the Box, and had decoded its mystery.

Both of them vowed not to divulge the contents to anyone and in so doing remained faithful to the Virgin Islands code of customs and tradition.

SNAKE AN' DEM

When he heard about the conflict between Mongoose and Guana, Rachy, the snake occupying the bushes in Corral Bay, St. John celebrated the possibility that Mongoose had finally met his match. He had heard of the intense quarrel between Mongoose and Guana and their reciprocal jealousy, but above all he was informed that his name had been invoked indiscriminately in the heated argument.

—"Ah hea' that Mongoose ben' braggin' bout how he help' de Virgin Islands government geh rid of deh snakes," said Rachy to a few snake friends. According to what he had read and what had been relayed to him the discord between Mongoose and Guana ran really deep, but again this was only his secondary preoccupation. Rachy wanted to know more than ever why the two enemies were so intent on talking about the snake family.

—"Ah ain famous, Ah ain infamous; why dese two keep mentionin' 'snake, snake, snake' nonstop; Ah jus' carn stan' it," complained Rachy. "Ah doan min' so much dat dey mention' us but dey portray us as stuiepid an' slimy…"

"An bad," added Rachy's friend, Alfa. "Wen Ah see dem two," she said, "Ah gon tell dem toh stap dat nonsense, stop beratin' deh snake…"

Rachy knew quite well the source of his real anger. The library had sufficient sources that accentuated the sordid history with respect to the two species: Mongoose and Snake. Deep down he hated Mongoose with a passion. Moreover, such hate was instilled in him from birth.

As Alfa was finishing her preamble, Mongoose was passing by, and reacted:

—"Yoh tink ah didn' hea' ah you? Look, wa' Guana an' I was discussin' was jus' deh trut 'bout ah yoh snake. Me an' mey family heh visitin' from St. Croix, an' Ah jus' wan' to clear up dis matta'. In fac', me an' Guana duz geh along real good now; we almos' like friens. He right heh close meh."

Jus' den Guana inserted himself into the conversation, "Rachy, Lemme tell yoh 'bout yoself…."

—"Lies, lies" retorted one of the snakes in the group, interrupting. "Ah you make up deh whole story."

—"Wait wait, Rachy an' company. Yoh tryin' toh say dat Mongoose wasn' imported heh toh geh rid ah you an' yoh serpent family?" asked Guana with a face of disbelief. "Yoh carn change history. Dey sen' in Mongoose toh geh rid-ah ah you disgustin' self."

—"Keep braggin', but lemme tell you, deh Virgin Islands people now tryin' toh find ah way toh geh rid ah you, Mongoose, dey sick of you an' yoh kin' so," objected one of the more aggressive snakes in Rachy's group.

-"One minute," said Mongoose, "nobardy want toh make yoh feel bad. Yoh read some story name' *The Unlikely Alliance: Guana an' Dem*"* and yoh suddenly actin' like yoh crazy. Guana and I jus' had ah disagreement over in St. Croix one day, 'cause ah doan like how dey look, o' how dey duz walk. Ah jus doan like how dey duz carry deyself. Plus, dey jealous of deh Mongoose. But, ah repeat, me an' Guana duz tark now. We make' peace. But, yoh have ah nerve toh be makin' comments 'bout we. Even deh congo dem prettier dan you."

The snakes were becoming angrier as they became more aware of the manner in which they were being diminished.

At this point, without hesitation Guana imposed his will:

—"Jus toh set deh record straight, partna'. Ah ain geh notin' 'gainst ah you snake, no matta' how strange ah you look. But frankly, meh really doan care much fo' ah yoh. It was jus' dat Ah doan tink dat Mongoose heh should receive any special award fo' gettin' rid of ah you snake. Deh snake ain notin' special. Dat was meh only point…"

—"Yoh insultin' us again," shouted Alfa "everybardy know dat we are the most dangerous animals."

—"Mey point is," continued Guana, "ah you ain as fierce as people tink. Harmless ting."

—"Ok, cum lemme soak ah bite in yoh, den tell meh if yoh change yoh mind," offered Rachy now visibly angry with the attitude of the two other animals.

—"Den Afterwards, come toh meh an' lemme bite yoh," added Alfa. "We will see how much fun yoh gon have."

The snakes were in the attack mode, ready to defend their honor as vicious predators. On this day their name was being reduced to mud. Everyone was changing their image and turning them into a helpless, defenseless species. Rachy, Alfa and those in their company that day were feeling the sting and animosity, especially from Mongoose. Psychologically their species had never been able to overcome the humiliation of the "Mongoose/Snake Project." And Mongoose with his constant bragging and arrogance was only making the wounds even deeper.

They could not take this derision anymore. They felt as if they were arguing aimlessly, resolving nothing, yet they must find a way to shield themselves.

"Tink wa' yoh want, Mongoose, an' you too, Guana. One ting fo' sure. We ain gon let you control us again. Dem days garn fo'eva' partna'."

Mongoose laughed so much after hearing that statement that tears were coming from his eyes.

"You belong toh us," screamed Mongoose;

"I agree wid dat," chimed in Guana.

Three islanders engaged in irreparable conflicts, waiting for just another reason to resume the discord.

In the bushes nearby there was a pack of mangy dargs prowling and listening, "coopin'"; it was believed that they were preparing to gain the upper hand in the echelons of Virgin Islands residential chaos and uncertainty.

*The title of a story in this collection.

FIRST CLASS TRAVEL

It was clear to all the neighbors that Alton's family was moving to New York City, or as every Virgin Islanders typically said, "*Toh deh states.*" The clearest of signs was the fact that Alton's mother, Miss Edris, had just purchased a brand new suit for him. Her son had never worn a suit before, let alone a new one, and was anxiously looking forward to viewing himself in the mirror. The dress code for travel to the United States was part of the unwritten law of the land, securely fixed in the islands' cultural signs. But in the 1950's and 60's travel to the United States from the Virgin Islands was no mere fashion endeavor. It was a real commitment. It took much planning and preparation. Miss Edris had already written and received numerous letters from her cousin Delma in New York. Alton had never met his cousins who were living in Brooklyn, but he had heard quite a bit about them. He had already been told about their history, living between St. Thomas and Tortola, their desire to move to the Big City, and their eventual love for the city. No one ever talked about the struggles of the immigrant families. Such thought would only serve to break the myth of utopia.

The family's departure was in a word, generic, in essence following the patterns of other eras. Miss Edris packed all the family's belongings and began collecting bags and boxes from neighbors, relatives, and friends who wanted to use her as their personal postal service. She did not complain, however, seeing this as part of the islands' cultural and traditional mores. In fact, she had anticipated that many requests would be made since she too had done the same when other families were relocating to the United States. No doubt, Miss Edris' years of saving pennies, nickels, dimes and quarters would finally yield fruits. The lore of the city, with its promise of economic stability and educational opportunities, was far too appealing for her to resist. But if history remained consistent, Miss Edris and her son's trip would be far from idyllic and utopian. It did not take very long for the Virgin Islands family to understand this reality. Their six hours wait at the airport in New York was necessary because her cousin Delma had to seek public transportation to pick her up. By the time they arrived at the tiny Brooklyn apartment they were exhausted, and nostalgia was already taking hold. The two-bedroom apartment was to be shared by Miss Edris, her son, her cousin and the latter's three children.

"Wey deh neighbor's dem?" asked Miss Edris of her cousin. "I wus tinkin' dat maybe ah cou' stop by some of deh apartments an' say hello toh..."

"No, no," interrupted Delma. "We doan really know each odda' like dat. Occasionally, the husband duz say hello. In New Yark we doan tark toh deh neighbors dem. It look like we 'fraid ah each odda'."

It was a very difficult social reality for Miss Edris and her son to fathom. In her area in Savan close to the Logan Church, she knew everyone, adults and children, even people living close to the market square area. In fact, she could recall long conversations with each one of her neighbors. She could also easily remember sitting in many of their living rooms with plastic covered chairs on which no one sat. Even though her cousin was talking to her about New York, Miss Edris was already daydreaming about the hens, cats, and dogs that would gather in her yard in St. Thomas on a daily basis. Animals with no known owners. She was in New York but was envisioning women drawing water from wells, hanging clothes on an outdoor line in cooperation with the sun's rays, and cooking on their coal pots. She was already imagining the aroma of the "fry fish an' Johnny cake." Physically she was in New York; psychologically, she was still on her small island. She could only reminisce.

"Doan look so depress'," encouraged Delma. "All islanders duz go tru dis." She was referring to the collective experiences- -of culture shock, of loneliness, of unrealistic expectations.

"Ah jus' want toh see ah few yard animals, an' Ah gon be OK," responded Miss Edris, only half-jokingly.

Her son with his sparkling new suit and tie bought on terms from the landmark *I. Levine Store* on Main Street, St. Thomas, was uncharacteristically silent. In his mind he was devising ways to convince his mother to allow him to keep on his brand new attire- - his first step toward his official conversion to Americanism.

Because jobs were scarce where Delma lived in Brooklyn, she was forced to seek employment in the Bronx. No doubt Miss Edris was imagining her own life symbolically prognosticated in her cousin's struggles. Noting this preoccupation, Delma offered:

"It is deh reality of Virgin Islanders in New York." No doubt she was subtly speaking of acculturation, economic pressures, and issues of identity. "But, you cou' make it heh," continued Delma. "The trut' is, Edris, many duz come heh an' silently endure conditions that dey wou' consida deplorable an' unacceptable in the United States or British Virgin Islands, or anywey else in deh West Indies."

Delma's words of wisdom seemed especially poignant for her cousin who just after a few hours was already experiencing feelings of separation anxiety, of self-doubt. Delma did not do much to alleviate Miss Edris' concerns, recounting the various intersecting stories of islanders lost in the shambles of their broken dreams. Miss Edris was already very worried about securing a job, earning her independence as quickly as possible, and seeking a good school for Alton. It did not take long for her son to be enrolled in school, but it was quite a few months before Edris could land a job at a fading watch factory in the Bronx, and later find a fairly decent apartment close to her cousin. In spite of the obstacles, this family was slowly becoming part of the social and culture fabric of New York. As Miss Edris looked at the historic monuments in the city she felt herself begrudgingly accepting her new identity.

"No mango, no guava tree," she thought. "Wey deh hills dem? Wey deh Fort?" All typically innocent reflections of new island visitors to New York.

Miss Edris and her son were now in New York, as she put it, "to stay fo' ah lil' while." In West Indian parlance this signifies permanence. Miss Edris, a very determined woman confronting her most inner fears and doubts, knew exactly what she meant when she spoke of stayin' fo' ah 'lil while.' She knew that she was there to stay, even though the first night Alton kept on his *I. Levine* suit as if he would soon return to the islands to feed the roosters and hens making noise all day and night in Deh Big Yard with the well and lazy dogs.

THE NEW HOME

They slept on the floors, an inevitable arrangement since the beds had their prescribed limits. The limited capacity of the beds mirrored the harsh realities beyond the two-room house made of wood. They came and chose the floor, or were chosen by it. Their names and where they came from still ring loud, and they saw Miss Maggie- - herself a mother of seven children- - as a person strategically placed in her house of limitation, a place where they could seek refuge. These men and women traveling to St. Thomas during the lean late years of the 1940's, 50's, and 60's came with one mission- - to better their lives and those of their families left behind. But it was a mission thwarted by and fraught with traps, economic pressures, geographic discrimination and alienation. Many came with no pre-arranged place to stay, others "sponsored", they believed, by reliable entities. Others thought that their contacts had been well established and were shocked to find out that no real contact awaited them. Yet, others were stunned to learn that their designated hosts had unexpectedly changed their minds. But they came nonetheless, to no cheering bands, nor welcoming committees. However, these new residents from St. Kitts, Antigua, Anguilla, the BVI, St. Maarten, Trinidad, Dominica, St. Lucia, Nevis, and other areas in the West Indies arrived determined to attain their goals.

It is doubtful if anyone in the Virgin Islands could accurately trace the cause of the xenophobic reaction, but it was clear that in general the same sentiment was not harbored toward the American visitor. They came, these Caribbean folk, and slept on floors, and hid to ensure that they would once again be able to sleep on beds with no flexibility. Those who

126

carved out their spot on Miss Maggie's floor, barely eked out a living in the public sphere. Their efforts, unregistered and unrecognized in the Virgin Islands, served as the base for survival for family members in the lands from where they hailed. Moreover, the intelligence, work ethics, variety of skills, diligence and resilience of these women and men were fundamental in reconfiguring the socio-political, economic, and cultural contours of the Virgin Islands. In fact, the hardships endured by these early pioneers were complicit in the crystallization of a new Virgin Islands identity, extending well beyond the geographic, sociological, and ideological markers that had been used to define *Virgin Islandness,* and in fact expanding new definitions of that notion.

Phillip had awaken early, at least an hour before the early morning sun imposed its will, sending heat waves through the cracks in the dark wooden house.

"Ah have toh be at mey boss' house by 5 dis marnin'," he said to Miss Maggie the principal dweller in the little wooden house in Deh Yard. "Dat's wen Ah begin toh clean he yard. Ah also buildin' ah lil' fence fo' him, among odda' chores in and aroun' he mansion. Thomas will take my spot tonight on deh flo'. Besides, it is my understandin' dat ah particula' ova' zealous immigration agent lookin' FO' meh."

"Sleep elsewhere fo' ah night or two," urged Miss Maggie, a uniquely wise woman, "he ain gon know wey yoh iz."

Thomas and Phillip were typical of those who changed residence on a regular basis to avoid the pursuit of immigrant officials. The uncertainties and fear of apprehension and deportation were never too distant from anyone's mind. However, they were transplanted by a strong sense of pride, the will to survive, and the commitment to the support of families elsewhere. Thomas and Phillip had arrived to achieve a goal- -economic mobility, or at least the hopes of beginning that process. Their determination not to yield was deeply embedded in a character fortified by the spirits of our African ancestors who resisted the yoke both on treacherous seas and lands. It was a character well reflected in the resolve of the two men. Fortunately, the main mission of many of the new visitors was also supported by some Virgin Islanders, moved by moral justice and the overarching notion of equity and fairness.

"Fo' mey family," Phillip would often say, "fo' mey family." One of the ironies of Phillip's earnest declaration was essentially what such migration did to families.

"I ain see mey wife and children dem in mo' dan two years," lamented Thomas one day. No doubt the situation was often very difficult. In point of fact, many single mothers left their children with grandparents, many of whom instilled in their grandchildren a rich tapestry of culture and tradition, ethics, morality, and an undeniable sense of West Indian identity, self-worth, and a prevailing sense of respect for all. In spite of this truth, in some cases such migration, forged by economic expediency, splintered families.

"Yes," remarked Miss Celeste one afternoon, "my children have benefited so much from this arrangement, even though Ah miss dem dearly. My mother in Antigua is givin' them excellent care, excellent guidance."

As a seamstress, on St. Thomas Miss Celeste had known long hours seated in hard chairs, and sweatboxes disguised as work places. A stitch at a time, she labored in isolation with constantly sore fingers and strained eyesight- -undeniable proof of her struggles. Sunday was her only day off, an important day of worship and a time to fellowship with friends, to write letters to her family and to reflect on her situation in her adopted land. Miss Stella, who worked as a cleaning lady also slept at the house of another family where she was caretaker for the family's children. She had come to St. Thomas three years ealier to seek her fortune. None of these individuals had much time for recreation. Like Miss Celeste, Miss Stella's mission was to plan and devise strategies that would eventually lead to the reunification of her own family. Her devotion and love for those left behind only exacerbated the level of anxiety of separation. But these new residents would not yield to the temptation to surrender, to return without accomplishing their main goal. Too many depended on them.

Undoubtedly, for numerous other pioneers, the sacrifices and the commitment to their families' welfare were non-negotiable. These situations epitomized that of many others traveling similar routes- — confronting and overcoming obstacles.

"Dis ain been no easy journey," commented Thomas, seated next to his friend Phillip on a small wooden bench in the Catholic School yard. Phillip concurred, shaking his head, "we hope dat our children appreciate wa' we went tru toh carve out ah betta' life for dem."

"We can only pray," added Miss Celeste, a woman of deep faith, who lived elsewhere on the island, a far distance from the two men.

"Only prayers, jus' prayers," responded Miss Stella.

Thomas, Phillip, Miss Celeste, and Miss Stella were talking about their early struggles in St. Thomas. There were days that they recalled with some degree of fondness, but there was also an unmistakable note of sadness in their eyes and in their voices, a sadness compounded by the fact that their stories are largely untold. There were parallel stories on St. John and St. Croix. Thomas and Phillip spoke one day and laughed, and wept and thought of the days when everyone wanted to lay claim to Miss Maggie's hard wooden floor, or that of another dweller of some dilapidated wooden house, in the United States Virgin Islands. They can laugh now, but they and other pioneers will never be able to laugh away the sore backs and necks linked to their sweet dreams and hopes immortalized on Miss Maggie's bed with no roses and the little house with its never worn-out welcome mat.

THE WILL TO BE FREE

"All un free in the Danish West Indies are from today free." Peter von Scholten uttered the words that historically marked the end of slavery in the Danish West Indies. The Governor General had checked the time and made the only decision that he could make, sensing the restlessness in the souls of the African Virgin Islanders, determined more than ever to claim their natural rights as human beings. After the appointed head of the Danish West Indies proclaimed his words of salvation, or so he thought, several citizens of Africa and the Virgin Islands were making plans to never return to that state of domination.

"Neva' again," shouted one of those listening at the site of the proclamation.

"Yoh so right" chimed in another, "and dis should not even be jus' fo' us but fo' the many dat will follow."

"You will be given your freedom today," shouted the man who wanted the people to be grateful and appreciate his so-called altruistic steps that he claimed that he was taking to better their lives. He wanted to present himself as a kind of savior of the masses.

"We doan owe yoh notin'," affirmed a voice from the crowd that wanted to remind the Governor General that freedom was inherent, natural, a right of birth. The governor did not seem at all swayed by the seemingly political declaration by the woman in the crowd who was quietly but assertively informing the Danish ruler that she was only "speakin' deh trut'."

The governor and his entourage did not take her seriously.

"Yoh cou' ignore meh all yoh want," continued the astute, persistent woman. "I ain have no concern 'bout yoh. Dis is all fo' mine own dem."

Interestingly, many others in the audience began to chant, many with words, and expressions that were remnants of various native African languages that they held on to for many years. Others were speaking in Virgin Islands Dutch Creole, a clear sign of the Dutch's economic influence. Still others, recent human cargo to the DWI, spoke exclusively in languages from the African continent. It was an extraordinary day of sounds, but ultimately there was only one language uttered in unison: that of the quest for freedom, emanating from the hearts of those who had waited too long. While the governor and his protectors patted themselves on their backs for their "humanitarian" deeds, those in the listening audience reminded themselves that it was their own efforts that guaranteed this day. Mr. von Scholten did not suddenly decide that there should be a proclamation. In fact, he and his cohorts were constantly hearing from some of the house slaves that something was brewing, that people were not accepting of their situation; moreover, they were not at all resigned. The governor depended on the house slaves for information, but did not fully trust them. It was a strange kind of arrangement, a paradox of sorts, played out regularly in the Danish West Indies. Oppressors expressed their mistrust of the slaves, but often entrusting to them their most precious treasures—their own children. But the governor had every right not to trust those house slaves, who after all passed messages to those who were planning revolt, revolution, or insurrection.

"Dey gettin' frighten'," said one of the house slaves who was secretly speaking to one of the most rebellious field slaves among the group.

"Dey gettin' ready toh break; Ah believe dat deh govena' plan toh announce sometin' important."

"Dey betta' announce somethin' big 'cause we ain gon take dis no mo," responded one of the leaders of the African Virgin Islanders.

This type of exchange was no doubt common among these people who had willed themselves to be free.

One determined and astute Virgin Islander opined, "some ah dem who write dem history books gon say how deh proclamation was because of deh govena' an' deh Danish people dem good graces, but Ah aways know it was deh people dem heh who wan' freedom dat fight fo' it."

"Dey had toh let us go one day," shouted a young boy beaming with confidence.

"Yea," agreed a woman in the group, "dat time is now."

When von Scholten gave his declaration on July 3, 1848, his audience of African Virgin Islanders were rolling their eyes "an' suckin dey teet', because long before the declaration was made, they knew that his words were inevitable. They knew that deep down that no enslaver deserved credit for returning what was illegally taken—one's freedom. The Governor General and his entourage had assumed all along that they would be received as heroes, as saviors of a lost people. They had underestimated the will of the masses that they had subjected for so many years.

Because they were blinded by their own notions of superiority they were unable to sense the mood in the air. The governor's attitude and that of the ruling class contrasted drastically with that of the subjugated masses. The ruling class, however, mistakenly confused the lack of power with a lack of will. The enslaved Virgin Islanders lacked the economic, political, and military might, but this was compensated by a high level of resistance and resiliency endowed by the African continent. The controlling powers were oblivious to the movements of conscience and the simmering disgust, anger, frustration, and the scent of revolt taking center stage in the underworld of the disenfranchised.

"Dere is sumtin' 'bout dat African spirit," yelled someone in the crowd. The truth is, there were spontaneous shouts from the African Virgin Islanders who were acknowledging the fervor of their own sense of self-determination.

"No one will keep us enslaved," shouted a middle age man who by the tone of his voice was not at all fearful of reprisals. It did not seem like the Governor General had heard him, or maybe chose not to respond to that fundamental tenet of the slaves in the DWI. After all, why should the governor and his cohorts be concerned about the powerless masses? The fact was, however, it did not matter to the man what Mr. von Scholten felt, or what history was going to record. It only mattered that the time had arrived, and no governor, no nation could alter the momentous shift and the move toward freedom, orchestrated by the victims themselves. No doubt, though, history, too often the enemy of truth, will record that von Scholten's moral imperatives led him to make the decision to "free" the people. Among the group gathering on that day in July, there were endless resonating voices, screaming in defiance: "We will be free 'cause we mus'."

"We demand our freedom," shouted an individual.

"Be free or die," a young woman said, challenging her sister and brother slaves to maintain their dignity and pride.

"Look arl dem people ready toh defen' deh rights. Dey come from Eas,' Wes,' La Vallee, from arl ova'. We doan owe dat von Scholten ah ting. An' Ah gon tell ah you, he ain owe we notin.'"

"Yea," chimed in a youngster new to resistance, "dey Dane people dem had a rough year; dey cou' sense dat we ah mean business. No mo' ah dis bondage ting."

The governor did not seem to capture the depth of this passion of any of these utterances. In fact, he dispassionately continued preparing his Declaration, emanating he would say, from a conscience committed to a humanitarian agenda. The African Virgin Islanders did not appear to be captivated by the official's interpretation of the day. They had already embarked on a journey toward freedom, one that had no pathway to return to a brutal past. "Yes, we mus' be free," reiterated a determined leader in the group.

Von Scholten and his band of supporters applauded his proclamation not because they were supportive of the subjects being "liberated" but because it had in their view the signs of future immortality for the Governor General. After all, this was a heroic deed that would alter the course of history. Among the masses was General Budhoe, Moses Gottlieb, who stayed in the background smiling, a snide smile that was proof that Von Scholten's edict did not move him the least bit. No other reaction from the proud and confident General, not a word. The General's aides, however were all laughing aloud at von Scholten's pretentiousness:

—"Because of my compassion I have freed all subjects," he spewed out to his audience.

—"He praisin' he'self again," whispered a young warrior just beginning the learning process of liberatory politics.

When General Budhoe could take it no more, he told his supporters that he wanted to set the record straight:

"Deh people ha done tell meh how tired dey was, an' Ah promise dat Ah would lead dem toh freedom. My promise is neva' broken. Wa Ah say, yoh cou' write in stone," he reminded everyone. "Now Ah heh listenin' toh dis man talk 'bout all he good works."

"But, he ain know wa' he talkin' bout," said a Congolese Virgin Islander. "General, you ha' don tell us dat we gon be free, an' we trus' you mo' dan we trus' dat man."

Budhoe smiled again, this time proud of himself, of his work in behalf of the people. His mission was to free the DWI from the ravages of a brutal system.

It was a day of much confusion with the man appointed by the Danish crown trying desperately to live up to his image as a compassionate proponent of slavery, an oxymoronic construction. Budhoe was well aware of the paradox endemic in this description, and sat there thinking of the false promises made to the residents of the Danish West Indies for decades.

The antagonists were accustomed to using smoke and mirrors to deceive and pacify the masses.

—"The Governor-General want toh talk toh you," said one of Budhoe's older assistant. "He say dat he was responsible for everytin' an' dat yoh tryin' toh spoil he record. Ah doan want him toh be mad wid you, brodda Budhoe."

—"Tell him ah busy," Budhoe said firmly. "I ain' geh no time toh waste talkin' toh him. He don know way Ah stan'. Ah doan plan toh change mey min' about notin' wen it come toh deh freedom of mey people."

A Yoruba islander expressed his concern for his leader, worried that the Governor-General would seek reprisals against their great leader for what he perceived as audaciousness and even more heretical, insubordination. He kept asking the general to please talk to the Governor-General in part because he knew that no one could fool Budhoe. Some had tried it in the past with no success. Budhoe was a strong leader, a determined Crucian who refused to compromise and who believed in dignity and pride.

"Maybe tis best yoh doan say notin' toh vex deh boss man," the man said somewhat fearfully. "He geh so much power. If he tink he is our savior, le' 'im tink so."

—"Mr. Moses Gottlieb. Mr. Gottlieb," shouted the exasperated Governor General. "I really must talk toh you today. This is an important day for your people."

—"Hea' 'im de again," said the Congolese man. "He say toh come si' down an' talk toh 'im, toh discuss man toh man he actions that will change our people life. Please, General Budhoe, talk toh deh man so he leave yoh alone."

—"How Ah cou' tark toh he 'man toh man', an he ain see me as no man? Tell him Ah real busy," responded the emancipator sucking his teeth and raising his head proudly, "Ah jus' ain geh no time fo' da man an' he stuiepidness. Ah yoh' ask 'im fo' meh if he ain hea' dem bells don ringin'."

THEY CALLED HIM CORNELINS*

(for my friend Ronald "Husky Harrigan)

Victor Cornelius and Alberta Roberts had no idea what was going to transpire that day in 1905. If they had a clue that there would be changes in their lives, they probably thought that those would likely be changes associated with local events on their island of St. Croix, Danish West Indies. Perhaps, there would be a trip to Bassin or some other area of the island. But on that fateful day something castastrophic was to occur, and neither the seven year old Victor, nor the four year old baby, Alberta, could have suspected that they would be uprooted, separated from their families, island, and friends, in one of the most underreported kidnappings in the 20th century. There is no question that what happened was not even considered criminal because of the ideology lurking behind the capture—the idea that these two black bodies were not of great worth. Victor's surname eventually was changed to Cornelins once he was in Denmark, but this change did not guarantee positive changes in his life nor in the life of his sister victim.

"Your children will be transported to Denmark to become educated and become good human beings," said the Danish man given the task of explaining the project. The parents, hoping for the best for their children, wished them God's speed as they were whisked away and placed on a steam ship, against their will and eventually ended up in Denmark. The children as well as their parents were powerless, economically, socially, and politically. That voyage to Denmark was a foregone conclusion.

"I don't want to go to Denmark; I want to stay with my mother," the little boy said, as he shed tears of sadness; similar tears were running down the face of the little innocent girl being snatched from her loving surroundings. The parents, blinded by the twisted promises and false assurances, had "encouraged" their children to accept the benevolent deed of the Danes.

"Why are these people staring at us?" asked the older captive who was accustomed to his folksy surroundings on his beloved island. "I don't feel good. I miss my mother." Alberta was echoing the same sentiments: "I really want to return to my St. Croix. I really miss my family and friends. No one is hugging me. No one is telling me good things. I am so sad." If nothing else, they knew in their souls that their native land of mangos, kennips, and cane fields was thousands of miles away. There was going to be a new reality, one that no human being should ever endure.

"Get moving you two. Do you think that you were brought here just to be idle? We have to take you to the show soon," said a man who seemed to be some kind of security guard wearing a brand new uniform with the Danish flag displayed as a small patch on his sleeves.

"What show?" asked the curious and surprised Victor, who at his tender age was very assertive. "We are supposed to be going to school, to learn important lessons. That is the promise that our parents were given."

"Ha ha," laughed the uniformed man. "Do you really believe that we brought you this far to be educated? You and your little friend better understand that you are here to entertain the people. Many of them have never seen your type. You will be doing a good service to our country. You will bring them joy. They would not have to leave their country to see subhumans."

The children, now intimidated and uncertain as to what would happen to them, had no choice but to comply with the terror that was engulfing their lives. At seven and four years old they did not fully grasp the implications of their fate, captured souls destined for a life of uncertainty in a strange land. But they had the sense that something deceptive had taken place.

"We are hungry," said the young boy who was serving as spokesperson for the two unfortunate children. "We did not eat a lot on the trip because both of us were really worried about our parents. We are also worried about ourselves. What happened to our friends and neighbors? Were they captured?"

"Stop complaining," shouted one of the attendants at the amusement park. "I do not understand why you are expressing such negative feelings. Both of you should be very happy to be in this great land. There is nothing attractive on your island—no good education, no food, nothing. You have nothing but wilderness and poverty. Is that what you want? So, you should thank God for this opportunity to serve us. This is not slavery. You are free to leave if you want."

"Free to go where?" asked the precocious boy who was quite aware that there was no refuge, no place to go. No place where two little children could go and be safe. Maybe they were not in chains, but they were unquestionably enslaved, being held against their will.

"I miss my mommy so much. I miss my mommy so much," Alberta would lament regularly. "I want to see my mother, want to hug her."

"Don't worry little ones; we have places for you to stay and you will receive that good education that we promised your parents," a government official tried to "assure" them, with obvious lack of sincerity.

The two children may not have had life experiences of adults, but they were quite convinced about what was happening to them. There was no question that they were the unfortunate ones, the bad lottery picks, chosen and sentenced to a life devoid of love and care.

Little Alberta was having trouble adjusting, not only culturally, but also with respect to the brutal winters in Denmark, the other harsh reality. She could not tolerate the pernicious climate, so diametrically different to her tropical paradise. Her death a few years later also spoke in symbolical terms of the suffering and humiliation that she suffered, perhaps the real cause of her premature demise.

"What happened to Alberta?" the fearless and insistent Victor asked the adults "entrusted" with her welfare.

"Oh, she died from the cold weather. It looks like she could not bear it, even though it was not really all that bad. Looks like she did not have the patience," responded someone who was hired to guarantee that the children were always kept under control.

"No, no," retorted the young boy. I know why she died. She died because she was lonely and sad. Yes, she died because of sadness and loneliness, because she was separated from her loved ones. Yes, I am very young, but I know that is what happened to her." In spite of his youth, the young boy had accurately and succinctly analyzed the circumstances of the little girl's death. Very astute for his age, Victor had clearly articulated what had befallen Alberta and what also seemed to be his destiny.

"What makes you believe that you understand this? You are no psychologist, no doctor; just a little Black boy. You are quite an abrasive lad. You need to respect your place—where you are and the benevolent acts of this community to help your depressed nation. By the way who authorized you to offer an opinion on this issue?" responded one of the grown-ups repulsed by what he considered Victor's audacious attitude, bordering on arrogance.

"I only know that the cold weather is not the only reason that my friend died. It was also because of indifference towards her, neglect, and mistreatment." Victor may not have known the exact words that captured the gloomy atmosphere, but there was no question that the idea of demonization and dehumanization was in his head.

"Shut up, boy. You do not understand the realities of life," shouted one of the officials disgusted by the boy's comments, and annoyed, maybe by the fact that he realized deep down that the boy had correctly pinpointed the situation. "You are not in a position to analyze anything. You are nothing but an island boy. In fact, you are nothing."

No amount of disparagement could discourage Victor; on the contrary he knew that he had touched a raw nerve. Nothing could deter him from representing the truth in the best way that his brief moments on earth would allow him to do.

Years later Victor Cornelius, alias Cornelins would become a celebrated educator and scholar, and a master of the Danish language and culture. In spite of the repression and oppression, he had achieved more than was prescribed to him and what the Danish community had expected for him. This child of the Virgin Islands faced evil with his eyes wide opened, and rebelled. His spirit of revolt and resistance marks a period in Virgin Islands history that speaks to the determination, resistance, and fortitude of two heroes who were sacrificial lambs in an adult game of inhumanity.

"I resisted it all," whispered Victor to no one in particular. "They thought that they had destroyed me, but my inner will of uncompromising morality superseded theirs. Their quest to silence me failed, and history has recorded the misdeeds of terror."

Alberta's sacrifices must never be minimized, and we must always honor her unwavering commitment to fighting unfairness and injustice. Together these two young people have helped to shape the Virgin Islands identity. If we bury them in history, we would be guilty of complicity in the most outlandish and outrageous international crime of kidnapping and violence in the contours of St. Croix and Virgin Islands history.

*Note: [The Victor Cornelius' tragedy is aptly narrated by this great Crucian himself.

My story given here is an imaginative trek, based on details highlighted by Cornelius. No attempt is made to recreate his personal narrative.]

DEH VISITOR TOH DEH YARD

(For my friend Edwin Davis)

Sister Esther had come into Deh Yard and retold her thrilling Zacchaeus story, of that determined tax-collector on his way to Jericho: "*He was a wee little man and a wee little man was he.*" Shoeless boys and girls, and shirtless boys listened in a yard that shared every inch of its dusty, sometimes muddy space with lazy dogs and stray cats. Poor Virgin Islands children listened to this kind missionary who brought the Bible to life, generally under a blazing and unforgiving island sun, and not too far from outdoor latrines shared by all.

—"*Zacchaeus had climbed a sycamore tree*," the gentle American lady would say, and her charges would sing in unison the songs based on the Biblical verses in the book of Luke and brought to life for small unsophisticated Caribbean listeners. Innocent listeners, too young to grasp the full impact of the lessons, mechanically mimicked the words uttered by the bearer of the Biblical tales, herself pulled into the middle of a Virgin Islands society still trying to come to terms with itself. These were islands still struggling to fully comprehend the U.S/Virgin Islands interplay, forged by an agreement between the Danish Crown and the United States. This was mid-20th century Virgin Islands, a relatively new experiment in U.S. expansionism. Sister Esther was admired and liked by everyone in the Big Yard, and her mission was mainly the evangelization of the little ones, the 1950's barefoot children surviving in an economically repressed Virgin Islands.

—"*For the Lord he wanted to see*," Sister Esther would say with her perennial smile, and American accent, and this was always followed by a chorus of West Indian sounds emanating from the mouth of babes:

-"*Fo' deh' Lard he wanted toh see...*"

Always in the near distance were the mothers attending their awesome responsibilities and singing Sister Esther's songs that they had mastered many years before this missionary even came to St. Thomas, probably under the tutelage of other missionaries. They were hardworking mothers of Deh Yard who were committed to their children's welfare in a stagnant and struggling Virgin Islands.

"Sister Esta' comin'," they would remind the anxious children. "Find ah box, ah bench, sometin' toh si' down on so yoh cou' hea' wa she have toh say today. Hea' deh word ah God."

No one knew how frequently, but they only knew that she came and preached and sang and smiled—that dignified American woman who brought moments of joy. It was happiness for girls and boys gazing at her board of pasted cut-outs that dramatized her stories. Today's version would likely be Power Point and videos a far different world to that of the shoeless children dreaming dreams that located them far beyond the Big Yard. Children too young to comprehend, never questioned the reason behind the visits. Analyses, whether social or political were beyond their reach, as they were primarily interested in their own happiness, generally guaranteed by their interaction with friends in and out of Deh Yard. "*Let us sing another song,*" Sister Esther would say.

"We want toh hea' anodda' Bible story," many of the children would plead.

"*How about the story of Samson?*" The saintly woman would then narrate her Biblical story, bringing it alive for the children of Deh Yard. Then the children would sing other popular songs, many learned in their particular Sunday school classes and reinforced on a regular basis by the visitor to the Yard.

No one could say exactly who Sister Esther was, and who sent her. There had been many assumptions, but to the yard children, none of them really mattered, even though at times there were questions which may have signaled some level of curiosity.

"Wey yoh from, Sister Esta'," asked one bold listener one day just before she began to prepare her intriguing Biblical lessons.

"*I am from America,*" the missionary would say, a phrase not fully comprehended by her audience. The children had heard of the United States, and some had even begun having dreams of going there someday. Some friends that they knew had moved to New York, a popular state of migration by Virgin Islanders. Many of the children were beginning to wonder if in the United States there would be a Sister Esther, someone to bring those Biblical verses and songs.

The new fledging relationship between the United States and the former Danish West Indies was beginning to create notes of optimism in the young ones whose world was inscribed by hills and oceans. But it was in this space, in Deh Yard, that dreamers began to dream. In a way, some of the optimism could be traced to the woman with the Bible who was dedicated to her mission, a mission not totally understood by her captive audience. But, Sister Esther was always welcomed in Deh Yard, and she came equipped to narrate the stories that the children of the sun had come to appreciate and cherish. They were the stories that in many ways created a different environment, removing them temporarily from their own meager means—bread and water days, days of milk and rice, of cornmeal pap. It was a tough world often disguised as culture, and recast as tradition. She came and rendered spiritual food, gratefully accepted by the residents of Deh Yard.

"*...the Lord came walking by one day, and he looked up in the tree,*" sang Sister Esther, supported by a cast of West Indian imitators, who sang with glee, with hope in their hearts. The children themselves now masters of the songs, sang them even in the absence of the missionary. Sister Esther had instilled in them some verses that spoke of hope. Like many of the cultural protocols of the 1950's and earlier, people were invited into Deh Yard space openly. The songs and the lessons forged their way in the children's lives, breaking their play routine. Without truly understanding the significance of the Zacchaeus story the innocent children sang songs of possibilities. These were songs that became part of their identity, children of Deh Yard, singing praises, laughing, giggling, and appropriately behaving like children. They sang without worrying about what their mothers would have available to prepare for food later that day, or the days following. Those thoughts were best reserved for the adults, for the guardians of Deh Yard. They wondered only about the meal that day, even though this stark reality was overshadowed by Sister Esther and Zacchaeus story.

Poverty has its unique ways of recoiling within itself in order to obscure truth and harsh realities.

REVENGE OF THE GALES

The runner had approached both gales as if they were largely inconsequential. He had described how he had successfully dodged large rocks on St. Thomas' south side during the reign of both hurricanes David and Frederick. The hurricanes, following the tradition of their more famous predecessors, of the 1950's, had made a relatively unpleasant visit to St. Thomas. The runner, Ronald, had insisted that his streak of 400 consecutive days of jogging would not be sidetracked or denied, and thus he would defy nature, jumping over rocks and carefully negotiating fallen electric power lines.

"These gales are not a threat," he had bragged in his characteristics formal way of speaking, while reminding his fellow runners of his unblemished running streak. It was during the latter years of the 1970's, and St. Thomas was still reeling from the wrath of the two dangerous storms. Ronald, however, did not view them from that perspective, opting instead to see them as "little inconveniences of multiple proportions," as he frequently referred to hurricanes David and Frederick. The runner was not alone in his assessment of these storms that were seen variously as "bothersome," "problematic," and "somewhat annoying." Ronald's evaluation of the performances of the two gales was akin to that of the art critic reserving his harshest analysis for a less than stellar act. He was a man of linguistic sensitivity who chose his words carefully and uttered them with a sense of pride. "These hurricanes truly disappointed me," lamented Ronald, articulating what many of his fellow and sister islanders had been thinking. In Ronald's mind, "the Virgin Islands are blessed, maybe because of our good deeds." No one has ever been able to confirm Ronald's affirmation.

But there was little doubt in anyone's mind that the hurricanes were not living up to their marquee billing, as vicious, fearsome, and predatory. Like Ronald, many Virgin Islanders created their own mythical space reserved for hurricanes:

"I will continue to run through them," the runner had asserted, supported by thunderous applause by a cadre of other runners. "These storms are overrated! That is the truth, and most people are just afraid to say so." According to Ronald's theory, the negotiating of a hurricane is a pseudo-science, linked to a sense of timing. He seemed fairly knowledgeable about his proclamations, and in fact continued to apply his theories about hurricanes until September 1989. It was then that a defiant storm, more vengeful and persistent than what the runner had experienced visited the United States Virgin Islands, and by its very presence challenged the runner's theories about hurricanes. Hugo, a vicious gale, in every sense of the word, took no prisoners, as it unleashed its bitter venom, especially on St. Croix. St. Thomas, also feeling its force and power, was also reeling as a result. In the entire process Ronald and others were beginning to question their own appraisals and understanding of hurricanes:

"I am somewhat afraid to run through this one," confided the runner one day with his penchant for language. He uttered these words as he sought asylum in a sturdy concrete building to escape Hugo's wrath. Little did he know that Hugo's actions were barely a presage of a more ominous storm. It came much later, bent on showing that it was no underachiever. Hurricane Marilyn came undisciplined and determined, or so it seemed, to silence Ronald and his band of soldier runners, slanderers of the Hurricane genre.

-"I am young," retorted Marilyn, born in 1995, "too young perhaps to truly capture the full extent of the disparaging remarks made about my ancestors, Frederick and David, Janet, and Cathy. But there is one thing for sure, Ronald and his crew of non believers and detractors will not be able to belittle my success. Furthermore, they will remember me forever."

Those words spoken, Marilyn lashed out, showing little sympathy and even less remorse for the destruction and disruption that she was causing.

-"Yoh rippin' nails from deh concrete an' upendin' our trees," someone shouted to the heartless storm one early morning, as the hurricane laughed and followed its sardonic laughter with a venomous burst of evil winds.

"Janet and Cathy[1] will be very proud of me," Marilyn blurted out to island residents and demanded that everyone stay fixed in their places of refuge, their prison homes.

Meanwhile, Ronald the runner could not understand why Marilyn would be so pernicious.

"Return to your place of abode, Marilyn," the runner screamed, now more out of fear, than disrespect. "No one doubted your strength. My comments were referring specifically to earlier storms, Janet and Cathy, some distant cousins of yours, I believe. In fact, I was not even sure that you were related.....I mean, uh…uh, it was all a misunderstanding. Uh… uh….

The man that easily manipulated language was suddenly being strangled by words themselves in the face of this forceful rage from the descendant of Hurricane Cathy and the rest.

-"Stop," interrupted Marilyn now incensed, and huffing and puffing while building up for another blast of exaggerated trade winds. "You disrespected members of my genealogical family tree; when you belittled David and Frederick in 1979, and Janet and Cathy, all of them, you insulted me. You must pay." It was an unforgettable night, and a rather rare conversation between the runner and the unforgiving storm. It was a night perhaps never to be duplicated, with Ronald pleading St. Thomas' case- -a case for mercy, and Marilyn for the most part ignoring his words and insisting on genuine respect.

"You know the adage," Marilyn shouted out to Ronald with the same derision that the runner had shown years earlier toward David and Frederick, "action speaks louder than words." Then another burst of winds, and eerie sounds emanating from the darkened, scary skies. Marilyn had

---

[1] Hurricanes of the 1950's

made her point convincingly. Ronald had sought refuge, a new believer of the viciousness of these storms. He quickly became a convert.

St. Thomas residents simply wanted a few moments of sleep. Marilyn's laughter of scorn and satisfaction of revenge could be heard from Red Hook, to the North Side to Bordeaux in the early morning hours when a very young gale forced an entire people to gain a new respect for nature's unpredictable and unalterable plans. No one suspected that two decades later, two more vicious, heartless gales, Irma and her co-conspirator María, would make land in the Virgin Islands, upstaging even the pernicious Marilyn, and reminding us all that nature is reclaiming its own in the most pronounced, unambiguous, malevolent ways

TRACKING GRANNY DEM AN' SO

(dedicated to all my brothers and sisters)

In Virgin Gorda they were preparing the best they could for the departure of the cane cutters finalizing plans to travel to La Romana and San Pedro de Macorís. No one knew how or when they would arrive, or where they would live, or if they would ever return to Virgin Gorda. But the villagers were saying their farewells. Jeremiah Stevens and his brothers were among the men planning the trip across the passage to seek fortune in a land unknown to them, but promising to lift them economically if they toiled in the fields under an unforgiving sun, in the shadows of those who not too long before toiled in the same fields without pay. They were peons in the thriving market of the sugar industry with its omnipresent perils. In La Romana the brothers joined with others from the BVI, the DWI and other islands, all clinging to the illusion of upward mobility from depressing economic communities.

—"Ah like dis place," Jeremiah said to his brother after arriving to their adopted land. "We will be workers in dis country."

It was a scene replicated through the La Romana and the Macorís regions. Unknown to themselves the men were putting in place the building blocks for a Virgin Islands diasporic structure that would extend well beyond anyone's imagination.

—"¿Cómo te llamas?" Jeremiah asked Edna Smith, a beautiful woman residing in La Romana. "Ah tryin' toh learn Spanish," he assured her,

149

while making every attempt to impress her. It was no secret that Jeremiah wanted to get to know her better.

—"Yoh say yoh name Edna? Dat is ah nice name."

—"Sí," responded Edna. "Soy de la Romana.....dat mean Ah from La Romana."

How could they know that they were setting the stage for a new line of Stevens family, from Virgin Gorda, to the Dominican Republic, to St. Thomas?

—"So yoh gon stay in La Romana?" Edna asked her new acquaintance.

—"Maybe fo' ah few years," the recent visitor responded. "God only knows. It depend on deh job dem heh; Ah jus' geh ah lil' job cuttin' cane. Ah have ah few tings dat Ah want to do on dis islun. Ah doan plan toh leave til' Ah finish dem. Dat's mey plan."

—"Plans duz change," Edna reminded him.

—"Ah know, but Ah stayin' heh. Ah have mo' opportunities," insisted Jeremiah the cane cutter.

—"Maybe me too," chimed in Edna.

The Dominican Republic offered hope to scores of men and woman migrating from the Danish, British, French, and Dutch West Indies, poor people trying to eke out a living a mere few years after slavery was abolished in most of the islands. Very much like the attraction of the Panama Canal in 1882, the sugar cane industry was like a magnet, pulling in the desperate and adventurous alike. Early century Dominican Republic was a haven for Virgin Islanders and other Caribbean neighbors seeking a more decent life. They were our ancestors availing themselves of all opportunities to provide for their families, in distant lands. At best, these were unpredictable treks, people moving to areas where not only did they not speak the language, but were not even sure if they had jobs. They were responding in large part to oral elaborations, rumors at times about jobs in the Dominican Republic, in Panama, and in Cuba. It must have been a highly competitive atmosphere with ambitious, hardworking men and women coming from every island in the Caribbean, sometimes taking spouses and children with them. But often going alone, a difficult choice that always put a strain on families. No one had been able to say with certainty where Grandma Edna Smith originally hailed from- -Anegada, Santo Domingo, San Pedro de Macorís, La Romana. However, her life and that of Grandfather Stevens intersected in La Romana, where many sought their fortunes.

The fast pace of migratory patterns during the first few decades of the 20th century dramatized economic urgency during that time period but also highlighted the exploratory spirit. In addition, however, it also created endless population shifts and constantly forming demographic paradigms. There is much irony lost on the fact that the Virgin Islands' embracement of its Dominican immigrant population in the 21st century is slow, at best. The surnames on headstone in cemeteries in La Romana and other places in the Dominican Republic hint at the story of inter-island migration. However, they do not offer details of the perils, rejection, of the challenges of the new identities woven and the new communities emerging from the juxtapositioning of traditions and cultures. If the Dominican Republic plan did not work, there was always Matanzas, Cuba with its miles of cane fields.

Granny Mary Moving had planned her trip for many years. She had made her contacts through the typical channels available to travelers during the very early years of the 20th century. The Danish West Indies for this Nevisian was constructed primarily through a collage of impressions from those who had visited before, or had spoken to visitors to the islands. Thus, her journey to St. Croix, Virgin Islands was first charted through mythical inventions and dreams. Later, the reality of the trip confirmed her unconquerable spirit.

Traveling the high seas, infested with sharks and other predators, was in no way a deterrent to this woman of small stature and huge ambition. The fact that she would do so accompanied with four small children spoke volumes of her indomitable spirit.

"I gon stay heh," Granny Moving had said one day with her characteristic pipe in her mouth and her inseparable hair tie. She had chosen beautiful Grove Place on St. Croix.

Granny Moving, Grandfather Stevens and Grandma Smith laid claim to geographical spaces bequeathed to them only through the inner working of their spirits of curiosity, determination, and vision. Their journeys, equally symbolic in nature, as they were real, made it impossible to essencialize Virgin Islands culture, and challenging to construct a clear picture of Virgin Islands identity.

"Wey yoh from?" someone asked Grandfather Stevens one day in La Romana. Not surprisingly he responded in Spanish confirming his linguistic acumen and newly forged identity. But, the truth was that Grandfather Stevens, besides saying that he was from Virgin Gorda, also probably wanted to say: "Soy dominicano (I am Dominican)," but struggled within himself to reconcile his present reality and his geographical birth place.

"I is ah Crucian, but Ah also Nevisian," responded Grandma Moving when asked a similar question by a new found friend in Grove.

"I believe I is Ah St. Thomian," Grandma Smith had answered when someone inquired of her identity. Ah might be dominicana too and Anegadian."

All three, however, were being re configured in realities which just a few years earlier were alien to them. Their clothes were barely free of the smell of the poisonous smoke from the boats, the mode of transportation to new lands. No doubt the fumes left their indelible scars in the inner recesses of their lungs. There was no time, however, to ponder health implications. Indeed, that can wait, they thought, as they negotiated and maneuvered their way to their new dwelling spaces.

Grandfather Stevens cut his cane rigorously and gradually became one of the best with his machete. For now, Jeremiah, and his brothers Edwin and Theophilus were staying. Edna, for reasons not clear to her descendants ended up in Charlotte Amalia, Danish West Indies. Jeremiah did not accompany her, but in 1916 their offspring Marjorie Asta Stevens was born in St. Thomas, Danish West Indies, leading to a new generation, started by Jeremiah Stevens from a little village in Virgin Gorda.

"I accept dis as mey new home," Jeremiah had declared, while sharpening the blade of his machete, already symbolic of the possibility of economic mobility.

Grandma Smith sat on a wooden box one morning in a yard in a place called Silva Dolla'. "Dis is wey Ah live now," she mused with conviction, and to no one in particular, but to anyone who was listening. It is quite likely that she also affirmed this in Spanish.

When Granny Moving arrived on St. Croix she marveled at the brilliant skies. She had heard a little bit about the island's glorious history, and felt immediately connected as she pondered her experiences in Nevis, her birthplace.

"I feel ah sense ah connection," she thought to herself, contemplating St. Croix's vast land space, and fresh air. The horse and cart had barely stopped in front of a small wooden structure, later to be called home, when the children jumped out. Their main goal was to meet other children and play; none of them was the least bit concerned with the trajectory that Granny Moving's life would follow. "That is deh business of adults," Granny Moving had once told them, words of advice that they had never forgotten.

Before the cardboard valises were unpacked the children were already frolicking in the yard in Grove Place. Granny heard their giggles and laughter and smiled to herself as she thought of the awesome challenge that she had undertaken, and the unpredictable course that she would have to follow. But she knew that deep within herself she had the fortitude to care for and raise her children, Nevisians and Crucians all.

"Ha, ha ha ha," laughed one of the youngest ones, totally oblivious of the fact that she and her sisters and brother were instrumental in the formation of a new Crucian-Nevisian reality.

MY ORIGINAL INNER TRUTHS

—A lead singer may have the voice of a nightingale, converted to that of an owl without his/her backup chorus

—Acknowledge those who touch your hand, cherish those who touch your heart

—Allow no one to define the parameters of your success through concocted notions of who you are or should be

—Arrogance inevitably breeds complacency, itself a blueprint for failure

—Audacity may at times disguise itself as assertiveness

—Believe in yourself, but do not become stifled by vanity

—Complacency will asphyxiate and stagnate you

—Compromise your integrity and begin the first step towards self-destruction

—Conceding your lack of knowledge is the first step toward a solid education

—Dig deep into yourself and witness possibilities springing forth from the well

—Do not be complicit in your own downfall

—Do not become intoxicated by the fumes of your success

—Don't be strangled by the urge to compete against others, challenge yourself, the most formidable competitor

—Don't dream of dreamers dreaming you

—Don't dwell on probabilities, but instead invest in the limitless possibilities

—Don't live trying to please your loved ones, but to better their lot

—Dwell on the past and be strangled by its tentacles of stagnation

—Educate yourself before you dare to assume the education of others

—Education begins within you

—Even the most dreaded curve in the road in the road of life, can lead you to a place where your dreams will be fulfilled

—Fail to recognize who you are and stumble on yourself in the darkness

—Faith ceases to be thus when effort and application reveal themselves

—Faith must not yield to pragmatism

—He/she who boasts of modesty tacitly admits arrogance

—He/she who shelters knowledge spreads ignorance

—Honor your family and in the process bring honor to yourself

—If you believe that education begins in the classroom, you have already begun the process of miseducation

—Inspire one person, then stand back and witness the magic of permutation at work

—Learn who you are by exploring the unchartered dimensions of yourself

—Listening is the centerpiece of the art of meaningful communication

—Lower the sound of arrogance to truly hear yourself

—Nature is recalling its own

—No truth greater than that which awakens your conscience

—One's greatest strength may well be the acknowledgment of his/her weaknesses

—Opportunity may not necessarily identify itself, introduce yourself to it

—Seek advice but ultimately listen to the voice from within

—Silence yourself before silencing others

—Silence yourself in order to hear yourself

—Tell who you are, less through words, but by the blueprint of your actions

—The first step of many steps may be unrecorded but it is the base for the later more heralded ones

—The individual who believes that he/she is "self-made" is delusional

—The loudest voice in the choir is not necessarily the best

—The most brilliant individual may well be she/he who brings out the brilliance in others

—The most deadly, ghastly fear, is the fear of oneself

—The only way to avert the atrocities of the past is to subvert the ideological traps securely set in history

—The stranger you fear may be yourself

—The suffering independent nation may well be in better shape than the overly dependent thriving state

—There is no such thing as a solo act

—Treat me royally and receive my gratitude, treat me fairly earn my respect

—Trust those who have proven their love through action; eye suspiciously those who only boast of it

—-Wealth is defined as the reservoir of unbridled humanity embedded in your soul

—-What is knowledge but the willingness to concede the lack of it?

—What is the past if not a barometer of the future?

—When the voice of reason and rationality is ignored, the door of anarchy and chaos automatically swings wide open

—Who are we? Coming from others who come from elsewhere who are coming from others coming from elsewhere?

—Your greatest benefits may well be those done for others

—Your mother, though gone, still is the rudder of the ship on this journey

—Your quest to comprehend the world must begin with your resolve to know yourself

Printed in the United States
By Bookmasters